TALL, DARK & DE WOLFE

HEIRS OF TITUS DE WOLFE
BOOK 3

BARBARA DEVLIN

De Wolfe Pack: The Series

By Alexa Aston
Rise of de Wolfe

By Amanda Mariel
Love's Legacy

By Anna Markland
Hungry Like de Wolfe

By Autumn Sands
Reflection of Love

By Barbara Devlin
Lone Wolfe: Heirs of Titus De Wolfe Book 1
The Big Bad De Wolfe: Heirs of Titus De Wolfe Book 2
Tall, Dark & De Wolfe: Heirs of Titus De Wolfe Book 3

By Cathy MacRae
The Saint

By Christy English
Dragon Fire

By Hildie McQueen
The Duke's Fiery Bride

By Kathryn Le Veque
River's End

By Lana Williams
Trusting the Wolfe

By Laura Landon
A Voice on the Wind

Titles by Barbara Devlin

DEDICATION

For Kathryn.

TABLE OF CONTENTS

CHAPTER ONE

London

June 17

The Year of Our Lord, 1497

A MELANCHOLY AUDIAL tapestry of death rose above the din of war, as vicious fighting reduced grown men to groveling babes, crying for their mothers or for mercy, neither of which would be found on the battlefield. In the midst of the conflict, Titus de Wolfe, son of Atticus, the Lion of the North and the patriarch of the estimable family descended of the great William de Wolfe, and Isobeau, savored the thrill of combat, heeled the flanks of his mighty destrier, and charged the fray borne of misplaced rebellion against the Crown.

In defiance of King Henry VII, the Cornish advanced on the Deptford Strand Bridge, to protest a tax imposed to pay for the war against the Scots. The sad thing was Titus agreed with the Cornish, because they shouldered an inordinate share of the debt, when the border incursions did not affect Cornwall. The tariff, unfairly levied, all but penalized those who had no stake in the game. Yet, no one asked his opinion on the matter, and he welcomed the chance to display his abilities and make a name for himself, because no one knew anything about him, beyond his legendary sire.

At center, the line broke, as the enemy, Cornish soldiers comprised of a piteous group of perfumed noblemen and clumsy farmers unaccustomed to such brutal work, offered no real opposition to the trained professional warriors deployed by His Majesty, and that dampened his enjoyment of the action. Then again, the great Wars of the Roses, during which his father rose to prominence, were no more, leaving Titus to carve out a place in the great De Wolfe dynasty, on his own.

After beheading one unfortunate soul, and dispatching another to the hereafter, he scanned the area, glimpsed the familiar De Wolfe ailette attached to a pauldron, smiled, and flicked the reins. "*Yaa!*"

A mountainous knight, an imposing figure in his armor, sitting tall atop an equally arresting stallion, waved to his armiger, as he led a forward assault flanked by the royal compliments of Lords Suffolk, Oxford, and Essex. When he noted Titus neared, the sad sack of ignorance drew to a halt and slid from his mount.

"Must you always make such a grand entrance?" The eldest son of Titus—yes, another Titus de Wolfe named for their ancestor, and Desiderata, Arsenius de Wolfe snickered and unsheathed his weapon. "As you appear better suited for the stage, cousin."

"You are one to talk." Leaping to the ground, so he could assist his closest relation, more a brother, given their years, Titus snorted and drew forth his two lightweight blades forged of Damascus steel. "And wherefore do you not bare your face, as that alone would scare off half of them?"

"Are we not the witty sort? And your lady declared otherwise when I rode her this morrow." Ah, it was an old insult, neither facetious nor serious, because they often competed for various women, but no one came between De Wolfes, and especially not the cousins. Adopting a familiar stance, Arsenius turned his back to Titus, in a display of trust that never failed to humble him, but such was the way of family, and together they prepared to fight. "How many would you estimate?"

"Perchance, two to three hundred souls in our immediate vicinity. Hardly seems fair." With his shoulder, Titus prodded Arsenius. "Are you ready?"

"Aye." As did Titus, Arsenius hunkered, in anticipation of an attack. "Let us play, cousin."

Enacting a graceful dance, of a sort, the two towering De Wolfes launched a lethal campaign so perfectly in tune as to render the distinctions between them invisible. As Arsenius, an expert lancer like his father, moved, Titus employed his signature skills, which he learned in Cypress, when he served *le Dauphin*. Two by two, the enemy fell, because no one could defeat the fierce De Wolfe duo. Thus Titus defended his family legacy but did little to establish his own prestige.

Therein manifested his weakness.

For as long as he could remember, he fought not a single adversary but, rather, the ghost of his incomparable uncle, an unrivaled warrior for whom Titus was named but could never equal. Betrayed by those who should have defended him, the first Titus de Wolfe was murdered at the great Battle of Towton, forever enshrining him as a legend in De Wolfe lore. It seemed no matter how hard the younger Titus tried, he could not match his long-dead uncle's prowess, and the failure haunted him.

The anger and frustration found a convenient outlet in the unfortunate Cornish soldiers, as Titus felled untold numbers. Ignoring pleas for mercy, he spilled the blood of countless men, until a sea of torn and tattered corpses blanketed the earth, and the Cornish surrendered.

"This was no battle." With a scowl, Arsenius shook his head and choked. "It was a massacre."

"I agree." Even his cousin unwittingly diminished the most meager achievement, thereby undermining Titus's short-lived moment of triumph and destroying any hope for glory. After yanking off his helm, Titus wiped his forehead and spat. As he assessed the enemy, a pathetic collective of boys and men with soft hands, he realized Arsenius was right. "There is no honor in such foul work."

"Sirs Arsenius and Titus, His Majesty summons you." Arsenius's armiger motioned toward the verge. "The King bade you appear with haste."

"Now what have you done?" Arsenius chucked Titus's chin, in a familiar affectation of familial camaraderie.

"I have been with you the entire time." As he

sheathed his swords, Titus pondered the situation, snorted in disgust, and shifted his weight. "How do you know the fault is mine?"

"Past experience." As he stowed his weapon, Arsenius arched a brow and snickered. "Were you not the one who seduced the Queen's favored consort on Shrove Tuesday, no less, which almost landed us a date with His Majesty's executioner?"

"You neglect to mention Lady Margaret, in the heat of passion, confessed a nefarious plot to overthrow the Crown, for which you and I were later knighted. How did the King put it?" Recalling the somewhat risky but pleasurable endeavor, which resulted in an unforeseen but beneficial outcome, Titus narrowed his stare and snapped his fingers. "Ah, yes. We are most right and true men in dedicated service to England, and who am I to argue the Sovereign's assessment?"

Despite Titus's glowing summation of what could have been a fatal event, Arsenius grimaced. "And when it came to Lady Margaret, you were quite dedicated to service."

Now that was putting it mildly, because he rode Lady Margaret like an unbroken mare, and he pondered his new target at court, a delicate woman with a smoldering gaze that told him she was not so fragile as she appeared, and he would test that assumption, that night. Winking, Titus climbed into the saddle of his destrier. "Indeed, I was, as I pursued her for months, but you are one to talk, after your bare-arsed jaunt through the royal stables, whither Lord Tabarant caught you grinding his wife's corn."

"That was a momentary lapse in judgment for which I have endeavored to atone." In that moment, Arsenius cast a half-smile, and his cheeks boasted a telltale shade of red, as he chuckled and reclaimed his steed. "Who knew that old, gotch-gutted, cream-faced loon could run so fast?"

"Well, in all fairness, you had your breeches and chausses gathered about your knees, which slowed your escape." Slapping his thighs, Titus howled with laughter, as he revisited the memory. "That was a sight I shall never forget, and I must say I feared for your future heirs, when you fled through the topiary garden with the thorny hedgerows."

"Cousin, believe me, I scared myself." Wincing, Arsenius drew rein, and they heeled the flanks of their stallions, in unison. "Yet we always manage to survive, because we support each other in our adventures."

"And just what manner of adventure do you have in mind?" As they galloped toward the royal tent, Titus glanced at Arsenius. "Ah, but I know you too well. What is her name?"

"Does it matter?" Arsenius shrugged, as they soared up the hillside. "What say we celebrate our victory with some of our favorite ale and fare?"

"Blonde, brown, raven, or redhead?" Hungry for the spoils of victory, and there was nothing that inspired a woman more than a decorated champion, Titus urged his mount faster. "Or does it matter?"

"One should never rush such an important decision." The King's guards stood at attention, as Arsenius and Titus neared, and that gave him pause. "But I believe I shall let Fate make that decision for me."

"Ah, a gambling man." Mid-chuckle, Titus sobered, when he spied Uncle Titus, who was, in truth, Titus's cousin. Owing to the difference in their ages, he referred to the son of the esteemed De Wolfe as uncle.

Born Titus Saint-Germain, it was on his mother's deathbed that he learned of his parentage. Later, in an eerie battlefield scene at Barnet, reminiscent of the betrayal that took the first Titus's life, Atticus rescued what he would later discover was his nephew. After a generous contribution to the local parish, and wielding considerable power and a will that would not be denied, Solomon de Wolfe formally recognized the onetime illegitimate issue, who assumed the family name and his rightful place among the celebrated warriors, earning a dukedom, in the process.

"Look yonder." A shiver of unease traipsed Titus's spine. "Your father awaits."

"That is not good." Arsenius waved to his sire, as he slowed his destrier. "Papa, we bested the rebels and won the battle."

"I would not be too sure about that." Uncle Titus frowned. "Come to my tent, as we have much to discuss."

Just then, His Majesty clapped his hands and admonished an attendant, which only compounded Titus's unrest. "We are not pleased that several thousand rebels marched to our doorstep, unimpeded, and we would have blood in recompense."

"Hurry." Uncle Titus flicked his fingers, and Arsenius, with Titus in tow, led his horse to the back of the line. "Step inside my temporary accommodation, as I require privacy."

"What is wrong?" Furrowing his brow, Arsenius

glanced at Titus, and he shrugged. "We successfully defended London against the Cornish attackers. Why is the Crown angry?"

"Do you really need me to answer that question?" On a table, Uncle Titus rolled up a map, tossed it aside, grabbed a chair, sat, and indicated Arsenius and Titus follow suit. "I suggest you take your ease, my son, as what I have to say will, no doubt, shock you."

The term of endearment evidenced all that Arsenius enjoyed with his father, and Titus envied the close relationship. Often, he wished Atticus treated Titus with the same affinity, but his sire remained distant, at best, and critical, at worst.

"Aye, sir." Arsenius paled, as he leaned forward and rested elbows to knees. "Am I in trouble?"

"That is putting it mildly." Uncle Titus rolled his eyes. "And when your mother finds out what happened, my neck will be in peril."

"I do not understand." Again, Arsenius met Titus's stare, but he was at a loss to comprehend their misstep. In silence, he promised to defend his cousin, if necessary, and they would face the executioner as they did everything—together. "If I offended His Majesty, in any way, I will apologize."

"You mistake my meaning." With a heavy sigh, Uncle Titus opened his trunk and retrieved a bottle, and Titus braced for the news, because his uncle rarely indulged in such habits. "Given your heroic performance on the battlefield, in defense of the realm, the Crown has bestowed upon you an earldom and a prosperous seigneury in Cornwall."

As usual, Titus's feats were overlooked, but that did not surprise him, as he was often relegated to naught more than a mention that he was Atticus de Wolfe's son.

"What of my deeds, which were equally courageous?" he inquired, with more than a little grousing. "Is my sacrifice to be ignored?"

Uncle Titus took a vast deal more than generous gulp and wiped his mouth. "The King also bequeaths a wife."

At the singular pronouncement, Arsenius appeared on the verge of swooning.

"Great abyss of misery." Relieved to have been slighted, Titus burst into uncontrolled mirth. "But you may take your reward, as I covet it not."

"I would not be too quick to delight in Arsenius's difficulty." Uncle Titus scratched his jaw. "As the King bequeathed the same to you."

"What?" Gasping for breath, as the world seemed to pitch and roll beneath him, Titus flinched.

"Now who is laughing?" Arsenius frowned. "But Mama will never support a union in which she had no say in the selection."

"Trust me, between your mother and His Majesty, I would rather confront the King, as naught scares me more than Desi's temper." Uncle Titus slumped his shoulders. "And Atticus may kill me, when we apprise him of the not so felicitous developments, given he and Isobeau are to host the weddings at the Lair."

"Well that should be interesting." Arsenius slapped his thighs. "There could be violence."

"No, that will not happen." Uncle Titus snapped to attention. "Whatever their station, our future in-laws will be De Wolfes."

"I understand, father." Arsenius glanced at Titus, and he feared he might vomit. "But at present they remain the enemy."

For Titus, that was putting it lightly.

⟫⟫⟩⟨⟨⟨

A WARM BREEZE kissed Lady Rosenwyn Burville's

cheeks, as she stood in the bailey of Tharnham Castle, her childhood home, which sat near the confluence of the Kenwyn and the Allen rivers, and a gem amid the untamed moorlands of Truro, in Cornwall, lifted her chin, and basked in the sun's rays. For the first time in a long time, she coveted hope, as she anticipated the return of her father and her brother.

After a rider brought word of men returning from London, and the battle no one wanted, because it pitted the Stanneries against His Majesty, she awaited a much prayed for reunion, given her mother's delicate state, in Papa's absence. The first familiar face to pass through the gate brought shouts of joy from the kitchen, as he was the son of the cook. But the mood quickly turned disconsolate, when he related details of the momentous loss and how the Crown's professional troops decimated the Cornish gentry. A sad chorus of weeping women dropped to the ground, while others offered support and consolation.

"What is it, Rosenwyn?" Mama ran from the main entry and shielded her eyes from the bright light. "Is there news of your father or Petroc?"

"No, Mama." Rosenwyn clutched her mother's hand, and they approached the gathering of servants.

"But I am certain they will arrive, soon. We need only be patient. I wager Petroc and Papa will be road weary but naught more, you will see."

"I hope you are right, my child." Mama squeezed Rosenwyn's fingers. "I miss your father, as he has been gone too long. In our two and twenty years of marriage, we have never been apart for more than a sennight."

"Vennor." Fearing for her relations, she tamped her anxiety, put duty first, and signaled the steward. "Send a messenger to notify those about the estate that we will gather in the great hall, and have the cook serve a warm repast, that we might mourn our brave dead, as a family. And we must reassure everyone who sacrificed and grieves a loved one that the Burvilles will not let them go hungry or homeless."

"Aye, my lady." Vennor dipped his chin. "I shall have the master of the horse dispatch a soldier from the garrison, at once."

"Gramercy." With that, she put her arm about Mama's shoulders. "Come, let us go inside, and prepare to comfort our guests."

"We should have a bath readied, as your father will want to groom himself, before he addresses our people.

Wherefore he insisted on joining the fight, I will never understand, as he is no warrior. He is a nobleman." Mama turned toward the immense residence, constructed of a combination of Cornish granite and greenstone, with tin accents from the streaming mines that supported Tharnham and its surrounding communities. "Indeed, I should air his clothes, as you know how particular he can be, in regard to his appearance."

"Perchance, I should change into my blue giornea, as I would honor those who lament." Just as Rosenwyn passed through the double doorway, a summons came from the barbican, and she glanced over her shoulder, just as a lone horseman galloped into the bailey. She would have known the black stallion, anywhere, and she spun on a heel. "It is *Petroc*."

"My beloved son." Mama pressed a fist to her mouth and ran to the growing throng. As she waved with both hands, Petroc slid from the saddle, pushed through the crowd of well wishers, and hugged her.

It was then he met Rosenwyn's stare, and what she spied in his brown eyes brought her to a halt.

"No," she said to no one, and her plaintive cry echoed in her ears, as she neared. "Brother, we prayed for your safe return."

"Sister, you should have saved your prayers." As he always did, he pulled her into his arms and kissed the top of her plaited coif. "As your pleas fell on deaf ears, and we were routed."

"Whither is your father?" With sniff, Mama wiped a stray tear and smiled. "Do not tell me he diverted to Bellesea."

"I am sorry, Mama, but I failed you." Petroc released Rosenwyn, dropped to a knee, and bowed his head. "Father is dead."

It was as though Mama were trapped in some invisible hold, as she stood stock-still, with her mouth agape, and then she fainted.

"*Mama.*" Rosenwyn reached for her mother, just as Vennor and two miners caught Mama. "Petroc, help me." Despite her entreaty, her brother remained fixed, and it was then she noted the tears streaming his cheeks. "Brother, it would seem you are now Lord Vael, and you must gather yourself, as our people will look to you for guidance and leadership."

"You are mistaken, Rosenwyn." Slowly, he stood upright. "I am no lord, and Tharnham is no longer my home."

"You speak in riddles, brother." She took him by the elbow. "Prithee, come inside, and wash the dirt from your face, as I have summoned our neighbors to partake of food and drink, that we might mourn, as one body of the faithful. And we must don the proper attire, to honor our father."

"I do not deserve a seat at the dais, or at any table, after I disappointed everyone." As Petroc stumbled alongside her, he gripped her by the wrist. "But worry not, Rosenwyn. I shall plot an attack, to protect you."

"What need have I of your protection?" She signaled Vennor. "When everyone has arrived, close the gates."

"Aye, my lady." The steward nodded.

"You are a fool, if you think that will stop the foul wind that blows on the horizon." Petroc wrenched her to face him. "Do you not see? The Burvilles are no more, and we live on borrowed time, at the leisure of those we call enemy."

"What happened?" Even as her heart broke for the loss of their father, she fought to maintain composure. Later, she would weep a river of tears. "Did the King not hear our complaints? Are we ignored?"

"His Majesty never gave us an opportunity to address him." Petroc bared his teeth. "He sent his knights, a pack of murderous butchers, to slaughter us. The only reason I survived was because Father insisted I ride at the back of the line. In truth, I never advanced in the conflict, as the Sovereign's soldiers cut our Cornish brethren to pieces, and our casualties were great."

"What of the tariff?" Horrified, she clutched her throat, as it seemed a horrible dream. "If it remains in effect, it could destroy our industry."

"Dear sister, I submit we are doomed, as we must pay the tariff and the King's penalty for engaging in rebellion against his authority." To her surprise, he cupped her chin. "And the cost is especially egregious for you."

"For me?" She blinked. "Wherefore?"

"Wait." Petroc glanced left and then right. "Come with me."

He pulled her into the main residence. In a side corridor, shielded from prying eyes and ears, he compressed his lips and took her hands in his.

"Petroc, you are scaring me." She shuffled her feet. "Prithee, do not keep me in suspense. What is wrong? What would the King have of me?"

"First, our father was stripped of his title, thus erasing the Burville legacy, and I do not inherit the earldom, Tharnham, or our mines." He swallowed hard, and she swayed, but he steadied her. "Second, Lady Senara is given to the enemy, along with Bellesea and its fortune, thus I have forfeited my bride-to-be. Third, His Majesty confers our property, in its entirety, to one of his brutish knights."

"What?" A chill slithered down her spine, and gooseflesh covered her from top to toe, as she envisioned her childhood friend at the mercy of some unknown villain and strangers occupying Tharnham. "Poor Mama, this will destroy her. And what is to become of us, as we are penniless and homeless, by royal decree?"

"Fourth, and worst of all, you are betrothed to the victor, as a spoil of war." When she gave vent to a dolorous wail, Petroc quieted her with an upraised hand. "Know that if you refuse the King's command, we are for the executioner's sword."

"The decision is final?" She shuddered at the thought, because her father always promised her some input in the matter. "I am to have no say in the choice of my future husband?"

"Have you not heard what I said?" To her surprise, Petroc grabbed her by her forearms and gave her a shake. "You are but chattel, and there is naught I can do to spare you what is, no doubt, a terrible fate. Indeed, you must do your duty, and there is no time to debate the situation, as we leave on the morrow."

"Whither do we go?" Grasping fistfuls of his tunic, she yielded to the tears that evidenced her broken heart. "Wherefore must we depart so soon? What is the rush? Are we not permitted to hold a service for Papa? Is His Majesty so cruel that he grants no period of mourning?"

"Our wishes do not factor in the Crown's decision, as we are but pawns." Again, he pulled her into his embrace, and she sighed, as Petroc had always been her champion, as well as her brother, and she admired him. "My wedding is canceled, and yours is to take place shortly after our arrival at the Lair."

"The Lair?" She sobbed. Was her fiancé naught more than a pack animal? "It sounds positively dreadful."

"I am sure it is terrible, but we must obey, for Mama's sake." With his chin, he nuzzled her forehead. "However, while I am defeated, I am not dead, and I will find a way to avenge our father's death and our birthright. But, for now, you must gather your things."

"Whither do we journey?" Shivering in the face of her new, cruel reality, she composed a mental list of various responsibilities. "Do we travel far?"

"Aye." He rubbed her back, and she relaxed. "We venture north, to Scotland, and a border village known as Wolflee."

"How awful." In that moment, she vowed to fight for her family and Tharnham, no matter the cost to her person. "Although I know it not, I detest it and my husband-to-be. Prithee, what is his name, that I might curse him in my prayers? And from what sort of people is he descended?"

"He is called Titus de Wolfe. Apparently, the De Wolfes are loyalists with a long history of service to the Crown, but that does not mean they cannot be beaten, and I am already formulating a plan, with my friends, to avenge us." Petroc gave her a tight squeeze of reassurance. "So have care, sister, and do whatever you must to survive, until I put Titus de Wolfe in his grave."

CHAPTER TWO

A SHRILL SHRIEK rattled the walls, as Titus's parents argued, with Desiderata and Uncle Titus waging their own battle, in the background, and Titus huddled in the hall with Arsenius. To his memory, never could he recall Atticus and Isobeau engaged in such fierce combat. Then again, never had Titus been betrothed. For a moment, he actually believed his father might strike Uncle Titus. A loud crash echoed in his ears, and he hunkered, glanced at Arsenius, and flinched, when a second thunderous bellow evidenced the continuing fight.

"Never have I seen Mama so angry." Titus tugged at his doublet and whistled, as the heated argument intensified, sending a servant running for shelter. "And to my recollection, the only occasion upon which she banished Father from her bed was after the feast of Christmastide in London, when he danced with Lady Arweld, but that period of atonement lasted but a small portion of an evening, as they woke the entire household when they reunited."

"I remember that." Blanching, Arsenius scratched his chin and pointed for emphasis. "Did not the King order Atticus to indulge Lady Arweld?"

"He did." Titus narrowed his stare, as he reflected on that particular mishap. Details mattered not with Mama, when it came to Papa's fidelity. "Do you really think that makes a difference when, as is the case with Desiderata and your sire, Mama reigns supreme, whither Father is concerned?"

Shaking his head, Arsenius grimaced. "We must never let that happen to us."

"Agreed." Despite his father's insistence, Titus vowed never to permit his future wife to wield as much power as Father surrendered to Mama. Of course, Papa loved Mama, and that was his mistake. Unlike his sire, Titus would keep his fiancée in her place, which was in his bed. Beyond that, he had no need of her. Satisfied with his plan, Titus rubbed the back of his neck and then slapped Arsenius on the shoulder, as they navigated the narrow passage. "Let us search out a firkin of ale in which to drown our sorrow."

"Cousin, you are wise beyond your years." In the

great hall, Arsenius hailed a servant, requested their drink of choice, and sat at a table near the back of the large gathering room. "Have you reviewed the condition of your new estate?"

"Nay." As usual, Arsenius approached his impending marriage as he did everything else, with a clearly defined plan of attack, whither Titus delayed his duties. "I suppose I shall survey the situation when I arrive in Cornwall, but I wager you have scrutinized every detail of the reports we received."

"Wherefore would you say that?" Of course, Arsenius had combed over each page of the documents assessing the status of Bellesea, in advance of his nuptials, whereas Titus postponed such boring tasks, as was his habit. Wherefore should he do today what he could defer until the morrow?

"History." A maid delivered two tankards of ale, curtseyed, and excused herself. "I know you too well, cousin." Titus raised his mug in toast. "To your marriage."

"And to yours." Arsenius consumed a healthy draft and gave vent to an impressive belch. "After studying the monetary impact of the King's tariffs, I understand why the Cornish farmers rebelled. They shoulder the greatest portion of the tax burden for a war that benefited them not, while His Majesty demands Lord Arscott supply the usual amount of clotted cream to appease the royal appetite. The situation is beyond unreasonable."

"Careful, Arsenius." On guard, Titus peered over either shoulder and frowned. "The walls have ears, and you could still land in the stocks."

"I know, but I sympathize with my soon-to-be in-laws." Furrowing his brow, Arsenius scratched his chin, and Titus could almost guess his cousin's thoughts, as Arsenius always harbored a weakness for the less fortunate. "They have forfeited their ancestral lands, their title, their industry, and their legacy. No doubt, they hate us, yet we are to wed one of their women. Their loss is our gain, and I would not rub their noses in their misery. Rather, I would welcome them."

"What do you propose?" Not that it mattered to Titus, because he was the victorious party, was he not? He earned his prize. While he would have surrendered the lady, that was not his choice, and he was more than happy to seize the wealth that came with her. Leaning forward, Titus propped his elbows on the table. "Most assuredly, they will hate us."

"Who could blame them?" In silence, Arsenius gazed into his tankard and frowned. On the wooden bench upon which he sat, Titus tapped a countdown, of a sort, until his cousin snapped to attention. "The answer is simple. We are De Wolfes."

"And De Wolfes always take care of our own." Smiling, Titus nodded, as he could have predicted that response. "How could I forget, when Papa recited that every day of the first twenty years of my life?"

"Although His Majesty considers our brides the enemy, the betrothals define them as family, and we must treat them as such." Regardless of Arsenius's honorable sentiment, which were much to his credit, Titus suspected that what his cousin proposed was easier said than done, because he knew how he would feel, were their positions reversed. "It is imperative we reassure our future wives that we are not their adversaries. Indeed, we are their allies and protectors."

"How do you suggest we achieve our goal, while seizing their birthright and their maidenhead?" Titus arched a brow, as the answer to that mystery eluded him. "Trust me, I am not sure which scares me more or presents the greater danger."

"Do not fool yourself." Arsenius cast an expression of unutterable confusion, and Titus struggled to suppress laughter. "The latter poses the most formidable threat, and I have no clue whither to begin, as I have never, to my knowledge, deflowered a virgin. Have you any experience with such creatures?"

"Bleeding balls of agony, no." At the mere suggestion, Titus wrinkled his nose, as he avoided the unspoiled like the plague. "I prefer skilled ladies, as opposed to chaste innocents, and I dread the time and energy we must expend to teach them the ways of pleasure. The poor thing will probably collapse in a fit of hysteria upon glimpsing my longsword."

"Mayhap we should inquire after our fathers for counsel, as they faced the same quandary on their wedding night." Arsenius averted his stare and scratched his chin. "Although I am not eager to broach the topic, as I anticipate a series of endless baiting, taunting, and feminine giggles."

"That is because their fair temperament hinders their ability to engage in serious topics." Wagging a finger, Titus snickered. "In fact, my father contends that every discussion of import with my mother ends in bed."

"No doubt the female penchant for emotion impedes their judgment, as I suspect the same is true of Mama." A strange assortment of countenances invested Arsenius's face, until he grimaced and smacked his lips, at which point Titus expected his cousin to vomit. "Papa often laments similar situations with my mother. Perchance physical relations offer the sole means of consolation when real world issues invade my mother's gentle existence, and she cannot cope."

"Well, we are the stronger sex." Titus nodded in agreement. "We would do well to take notes for future reference, that we might provide succor in like fashion. You know me, I will take any excuse to drain my moat."

"Oh, do I know you." Laughing, Arsenius stared at the contents of his tankard. "I wonder if I might ask you a personal question."

"When have you not?" Titus snorted. "We have no secrets, cousin. I am your brother, as you are most assuredly mine."

"I wondered if you embrace the opportunity the King bestowed upon us?" Shifting his weight, Arsenius voiced Titus's innermost vulnerability. Given Arsenius's close relationship with his father, Titus never imagined his cousin shared the same feelings, in regard to their inescapable lineage. "Do you never find yourself alone amid our family? Are you never lost in the crowd? Have you ever wished that you might journey some place whither—"

"—No one knows my name?" Titus could scarcely believe his ears, as he locked forearms with Arsenius. "Whither no one has heard of the De Wolfe legacy?"

"Aye." The relief in Arsenius's expression mirrored Titus's, and it dawned on him that no one could better relate to the never-ending expectations than someone in the same position. Indeed, Arsenius had a celebrated sire with which to contend. "Forgive me, if this offends you, but I am excited about the prospect of moving to Cornwall and forging my own heritage. And although I do not yet know the character of my bride-to-be, I am emboldened by the possibilities associated with the title and estate."

"I, too, am blessed with renewed vigor and a spirit of adventure I have not experienced since Father hired my first whore." So, Titus did not use the same elegant terms to express his emotions. Then again, with Arsenius, Titus could always be himself. "Ah, I have fond recollections of her red hair and the funny little sounds she made in the throes of passion. What was she called?"

"How should I know?" Compressing his lips, Arsenius averted his gaze. "And I wager her passion relied more on Atticus's generous payment than your fledgling abilities between the sheets."

"Do not insult my skills, cousin." Titus sobered, as he took the bait his cousin foolishly dangled. "Though you have grown to equal my size, I can still whip you."

"Is that so, old man?" Arsenius gulped the last of his ale, set down the tankard with a loud thud, and stood. "I would like to see you try."

Without warning, not that he ever extended such courtesies; Titus lunged across the table and grabbed his cousin by the throat. Moving swift and sure, just as Titus anticipated, Arsenius stretched high but then tripped Titus, and they toppled to the ground. That was a sharp move he would not forget. Rolling left and then right, with each gaining the high ground for a moment, before the other made a successive launch, they knocked over and reduced a bench to splinters, chuckling the entire time. He rumpled Arsenius's hair, and he pinched Titus's nose, until someone coughed rather loudly.

"What goes on hither?" Folding his arms, Atticus glared at Titus and then Arsenius. "It appears a couple of braying asses have ventured into the great hall."

"Mayhap a visit to the sanctuary and an afternoon spent in reflective prayer will do them some good." Adopting a similar portentous stance, Uncle Titus bared his teeth. "But first my son will right his clothing and comb his hair, that he might greet his future wife in a manner befitting a De Wolfe, as her traveling party is just arrived."

"Yes, Father." Arsenius shuffled to his feet, turned, and extended a hand, which Titus accepted. "Apologies, cousin. I should not have charged you."

"And, as the eldest, he should not have engaged you." No, it did not surprise Titus that his father criticized him. "Thus my son owes you the apology."

"That is not necessary." Arsenius slapped Titus on the back. "After all, we are family."

"But it is, according to the great Lion of the North." Titus gritted his teeth and then bowed, with a flourish, to further irritate his father. "Dear cousin Arsenius, I humbly beg your forgiveness for my shameful behavior, good sirrah."

"*Enough.*" Father folded his arms. "I will speak with you in the solar—now."

"Of course." With a swagger, Titus held high his chin and marched to the master's chamber, whither he would endure another lecture on honor and duty. "Shall I save you the time and trouble and recite the usual oratory, to myself? I can use the long mirror in my quarters and adopt your stance."

"You will hear what I have to say, and then you will present yourself in the bailey, to greet your cousin's betrothed." In the solar, Father slammed shut the door. "And you will do naught to embarrass the De Wolfe name."

"Wherefore do you not admit that my very existence is an embarrassment to the De Wolfes?" Tired of games he no longer wished to play, Titus smacked a fist to a palm. "If you prefer, I will refuse the King's command, and then you would never again have to look upon my face, as I have disappointed you so."

"Wherefore do you speak such nonsense?" Whereas Titus thought his father would relish the opportunity to rid himself of his mistake, Papa seemed shocked. "You are my son, and I love you."

Titus searched for a ribald reply, anything to break

free of the invisible prison manifested by his father's declaration, but he could form no response. Indeed, he simply stood there, as Papa wrapped his arms about Titus.

"Regardless of what I do, no matter how many battles I fight, I can never live up to your deeds." As he did as a child, Titus rested his head to his father's shoulder and found long absent comfort. "I am sorry that I failed you, but it is not easy being your son."

"You think you tell me something I know not?" Father released Titus and retreated a step. "I am the son of Solomon De Wolfe, and we are all descended of the famed William De Wolfe. However, we cannot live in the shadow of great men, as they are gone and have passed into the annals of history. They benefit from human forgetfulness, as we only recall their triumphs and not their failures. As the living, we can only do our best, forge our own path, and be satisfied with the outcome. For you, I want naught but your happiness, which you must define, for yourself. Find that, and you will be a success, my son."

"Wherefore have you never said these things to me, ere now?" Titus stretched tall and met his father's stare. "Wherefore did you not talk to me?"

"Because I did not see you as a man, until now." Papa grinned and shook his head. "I suppose it is because you are about to take a wife. But to me, you will always be my son, who used to cling to my legs whenever I returned to the Lair. There is much more I would say, but we must receive the Arscotts, so our discussion must wait, until the morrow, ere you take your vows. Today, you must prepare yourself to stand at my side, as my firstborn. As my heir. One day, all this will be yours, when you take my place as master of the Lair."

"I will, Father." With much to ponder, Titus wiped his brow and considered Arsenius's advice, as well as Papa's words of encouragement. "But I could only succeed you."

⟫⟫⟫⟪⟪⟪

IT WAS DAWN as the Burville traveling coach navigated the Scottish village, climbed the vast expanse, and crossed the bridge of the Lair, high atop Wolflee Hill, conveying Rosenwyn to her doom. At the massive, wrought iron portcullis, the equipage slowed, and from the barbican, several soldiers took up arms, as though the enemy advanced. So that was how the De Wolfe's welcomed her.

"Who seeks passage?" a guard inquired.

"The Burvilles." Petroc cast a dour frown, mirroring her mood, which had only deteriorated since they departed Tharnham, given Mama constantly wept. "We bring Lady Rosenwyn to her wedding."

"Of course, my lord." The guard whistled, and the huge wood panel creaked and groaned. "The honorable Sir Atticus De Wolfe expects you. Welcome to the Lair."

In the bailey, servants and soldiers rushed in all directions, and a line composed of elegantly dressed ladies and knights formed at the entry to the impressive residence. As she descended to the gravel surface, she swayed, and Petroc offered support.

"I do not think I can do this, brother." Her knees buckled, as a mountainous figure of a man charged forth, to steady her, and she wanted to scream. Piercing blue eyes seemed to cut through her, when they touched, and she stumbled back, but he held fast. "I beg your pardon. Unhand me, sir."

"Let go of my sister." Petroc rose to her defense, but the mountain brushed aside her brother, as though he were naught but a feather.

"Easy, Burville, as I mean no offense." The mountain gave her his full attention, and she admired his chiseled, patrician features and thick brown hair. "Lady Rosenwyn, I presume?" The scourge had the audacity to address her.

"Indeed." She tried but failed to wrench free and pitied any woman who had to deal with the mountain on a regular basis. "And I do not believe we are acquainted."

"Apologies, if I frightened you, but you appeared on the verge of fainting. Permit me to introduce my parents and the masters of the Lair." He pointed to a distinguished couple. "I present my father, the Lion of the North, Sir Atticus de Wolfe, and my mother, Lady Isobeau." Still clutching her fingers, the mountain clicked the heels of his boots and bowed. "And I am Sir Titus de Wolfe, your fiancé."

In that instant, Rosenwyn yielded to a black veil of silence.

Floating in some strange yet comforting pall of darkness, she thought someone called her name, but she could not respond. Little by little, the fog cleared, and she discovered herself reclining in a bed, with Mama at one side and Lady Isobeau at the other.

"What happened?" When Rosenwyn attempted to sit upright, everything spun out of control, and she doubled over. "Prithee, tell me I did not embarrass myself and my family."

"Have care, child." Offering naught but kindness, Lady Isobeau pressed a cool cloth to Rosenwyn's forehead. "My son gave you quite a shock, and I will have words with him, as he knows better."

In a rapid assault on her senses, a series of images flashed before her, all centering on the mountain that was to be her husband, and the room seemed to spin ever faster, thus she clutched the bedclothes. "*Oh.*"

"Hither, my dear." Mama held a goblet. "Have some water, as it will refresh you."

"I do not want water, Mama." Rosenwyn brushed aside the cloth, as Lady Isobeau fluffed a pillow. "I should like to replay our arrival, sans the swooning and my resulting shame. How can I show my face after this?"

"I am afraid there is no time to mull the question, as Lady Senara's wedding to my nephew, Sir Arsenius, takes place before the noon meal, and you must dress for the ceremony." Lady Isobeau inclined her head and smiled. "But I can assure you no one thinks ill of you,

Lady Rosenwyn, so you need not fret. Shall I send my attendant to help you change?"

"Thank you, Lady Isobeau." Rosenwyn nodded, as she scooted to the edge of the mattress.

Somehow, in the midst of the unsettling developments, she forgot about her childhood friend who shared the same fate. Regardless of her fears and hesitation, she had to support Senara.

After donning a black kirtle, with a V-neck, which she filled with a sheer linen partlet, to preserve her modesty, and a fur-trimmed, burgundy giornea bedecked in old gold, Rosenwyn sat before the long mirror, as the servant affixed a bejeweled wimple.

Satisfied with her appearance, she stood, smoothed her skirt, and inhaled a deep breath. Rolling her shoulders, she walked to the portal, grasped the iron ring, and opened the door.

In the hall, she found her mother and Lady Isobeau.

"Lady Rosenwyn, you are a vision, and I am certain my son will count himself fortunate to have you for a wife." Lady Isobeau extended a hand and flicked her fingers. "Anon, let us away, as the wedding party has already departed for the chapel."

"Am I to ride with Sir Titus?" Rosenwyn braced for the possibility, as her husband-to-be terrified her.

"Nay, child." Lady Isobeau giggled. "He accompanied his cousin to the chapel, so you need not worry about another exchange."

"I am so sorry, if I offended your family, Lady Isobeau." Rosenwyn trailed in the noblewoman's wake. "But I know not what to make of him, and he can be rather provoking."

"That is putting it mildly." As Lady Isobeau descended the stairs, she peered over her shoulder. "My dear, De Wolfe men are no real mystery. For all their size, bluster, and aggression, the *great warrior knights* are but simple creatures in possession of two elementary needs, which define them, through and through." The emphasis in Lady Isobeau's voice gave Rosenwyn pause, and she yielded to nervous laughter. "The first resides in their bellies. The second...well, I gather your mother has discussed the requisite duties associated with the marriage bed. Satisfy both demands, and you will have no difficulties managing my son."

"Indeed?" Given Isobeau's bold statement, Rosenwyn feared she might faint, again. The only problem was Mama neglected to enlighten Rosenwyn on that particular aspect of the marital relationship. To her chagrin and mortification, she knew naught of her future husband's expectations, in that respect, and her mind ran wild with all manner of torturous assumptions, which wreaked havoc on her composure, and she tripped, as they walked into the bailey.

"Rosenwyn, are you all right?" Mama frowned and then drew near. "In our haste to depart Cornwall, I did not consider the intimate details of your impending wedding. Mayhap this eventide, we can explore the more delicate aspects of your future union and the services you must render."

"Gramercy, Mama." On the outside, Rosenwyn fought to convey an air of confidence, but on the inside she trembled, as she stepped into the coach.

Her father promised that, when the time came to select a match for his only daughter, he would allow her some influence. His Majesty honored no such pledge, and her desires factored not, in the end. One thing was certain; she never would have picked a man like Titus de Wolfe.

The mountain, as she thought of him, posed danger unlike any she had ever confronted, and she knew not how to handle him, despite Lady Isobeau's assurances.

As Rosenwyn joined the family, in the chapel, she craned her neck to gain sight of Lady Senara.

To Rosenwyn's horror, her friend confronted another enormous male specimen, who stood at equal height to Sir Titus. As the couple clasped hands, and the ceremony commenced, she could not contain her tears. When she surveyed the crowd, she met Titus's stare and almost shrieked. Wherefore did he watch her? Slowly, he smiled, and she leaped to her feet.

Ere she disrupted the event; she retreated to the rear and fled to a narrow corridor, which led to a second smaller sanctuary. At the tiny altar, she collapsed to her knees and bit the fleshy underside of her hand to stifle her sobs of misery.

"Lady Rosenwyn, are you unwell?" At Titus's prompt, she sat on her ankles and wiped her cheeks, with the back of her hand. "Shall I escort you to your chambers?"

"Wherefore do you want me?" Without care for her person, she challenged her adversary. "Wherefore does Sir Arsenius want Lady Senara? She is my friend. I have known her all my life. We grew up together. She was to marry my brother and become my sister, in truth, and now it is all gone. Wherefore, I ask you?"

"Because His Majesty decrees otherwise, my lady." To her shock, which seemed the usual state with her fiancé, he squatted beside her, which only emphasized the difference in their sizes. "And as the King's knight, I am honor bound to obey."

"Is that how you go about your life?" Regardless of his beauteous face, she longed to hate him, and she summoned ire at the unfairness of her betrothal. "You obey the King's edicts, without protest? Have you no will of your own? What manner of man are you?"

"One that understands duty, my lady." When Titus reached for her, she flinched. "You fear me."

It was a statement, not a question.

"Of course, I fear you." Recalling the nuptials taking place in the nave, she lowered her voice. "For all I know, you killed my beloved father. You stood against a group of nobles, farmers, and miners, when their cause was right and true, and you slaughtered them."

"Lady Rosenwyn, as you are to be my wife, I am no threat to you." When guests lingered in the hall, he caught her about the waist, lifted her as he stood, and carried her to the corner, shielded from view. As she made to object, he pressed a finger to her lips. "Shh. Unless you want an audience."

"Nay." In such close confines, she could not help but study her fiancé. Under other circumstances, she might have found him a suitable husband, but not when she was forced to the altar. "Neither do I welcome your company."

"I cannot blame you, as I felt the same way, when I was informed of what His Majesty considers my good fortune." With tenderness of which she thought him incapable, he caressed her cheek. "But I am not ignorant to the fact that my reward comes at your expense, and I would make amends, if you permit it."

"How?" What he proposed struck her as impossible. "Sir Titus, at the risk of offending you, I do not trust you."

"That is understandable, and I bear no ill will, my lady." Even though they eluded discovery, he held her in his unrelenting embrace. "While I am sure you never could have anticipated the outcome of the battle, I have always known that my bride would be chosen for me, not by me, as I serve at the King's leisure. I wed by his commission."

"Do you wish to marry me?" Wherefore she posed the query she knew not, but his answer would determine her course of action.

"Aye." When she gasped, he chuckled. "My lady, let me assure you, I did not harbor such sentiment when I first learned of my fate."

"Oh?" Perchance they shared more in common than Rosenwyn realized. "What swayed your thinking?"

"You." In that moment, he lifted her higher, bringing them nose-to-nose, and she pressed her palms to his chest. "As I said, I never expected my wishes to factor in the Crown's selection of my bride, but I am grateful for His Majesty's choice, because you are quite beauteous, Lady Rosenwyn, if I may be so bold. But more than your appearance, I value your spirit, which you evidence in your undeniable honesty. In short, a De Wolfe has no need of a simple wife. Rather, he wants a partner, and I believe you more than capable, thus you fulfill my standards, in every way."

"But you hardly know me." Yet, she could not argue his position, when they aligned so perfectly with hers. "And as I said, how can I trust you?"

"Dear lady, that will come in time, as I get to know you, and you get to know me." Something in his demeanor told her that he referred to more than everyday habits and favorite foods, and she shivered.

"For now, let us join the wedding celebration, as the ceremony is ended. And I suggest you rest, this eventide, as we marry, on the morrow, and begin our life, together."

CHAPTER THREE

THE SUN PEEKED above the horizon, on his wedding day, as Titus stood before the lancet window in the solar and tugged at his black tunic, which matched his mood, as so much remained unsettled between him and his bride-to-be. As he pondered Lady Rosenwyn's response to his proposal, he also reflected on the advice given by his mother and Aunt Desi, none of which inspired confidence.

How was he to make sense of the nonsensical?

"Nervous, cousin?" When Titus peered over his shoulder, he discovered Arsenius standing in the doorway. That was just what he needed, a thorn in his side, to distract him, as he prepared to take his vows. "Planning to flee the ceremony?"

"I am still surprised you made it to yours, and what are you doing hither?" Titus snickered, as he honed a rapier retort. "I thought you would be busy with your new wife, but you look rather rested for a fledgling husband. Bored so soon, or did she banish you from her bed, already?"

"Not that it is any of your affair, but I granted my nervous young bride a deferment, as our mothers suggested, that Senara and I might know each other before we *know* each other, and she was grateful." Folding his arms, Arsenius arched a brow and appeared a little too pleased with himself. "It is called consideration. You should try it, you abyss of unknowing."

"What is this?" Father entered the solar, along with Uncle Titus. "Must we separate you, as we would two mischievous children?"

"Nay, Father." In play, Titus punched his cousin in the shoulder, which harkened to cherished days of old. "Arsenius was just offering his usual, unfailing support."

"Is that so?" Uncle Titus cast an expression of pure skepticism. "And wherefore is my son imparting unsolicited advice, when he should be tending his bride, given his young tenure as a spouse?"

"Especially since your last suggestion yielded naught but an upset belly and visions I may never erase from my mind, which haunted me in slumber." Titus recalled the conversation with their mothers, on the eve of Arsenius's wedding, concerning the deflowering, which failed miserably, and he swallowed hard. "You should be whipped for that gem of insanity."

"If I remember correctly, you thought it a brilliant plan, at the time." Arsenius scowled, and Titus scored a direct blow. "How was I to know our mothers would find sport in our queries?"

"What is this?" Father glanced at Uncle Titus, and it was too late when Titus realized his misstep. "They sought the counsel of our wives, when we were available? Are we not thriving husbands?"

Arsenius rolled his eyes.

"Indeed, so it appears." Uncle Titus rubbed the back of his neck and said to Arsenius, "To what end did you consult with your mother?"

Perchance, if Titus were lucky, Arsenius knew better than to admit the truth.

"We wanted to know how best to achieve the consummation with our virgin brides, to foster amity, as opposed to fear." Bowing his head, Arsenius shuffled his feet, and Titus was not so lucky, after all. "As neither of us possesses much experience with such creatures."

"Oh?" Uncle Titus thrust his chest, when Arsenius hesitated. "Well, out with it. What did your mama have to say on the matter?"

Desperate, Titus attempted to stem the tide. "It is not what you suppose, as they did not—"

"That you were nervous." Arsenius cleared his throat, and Titus winced. "And you would not stop talking."

Father burst into laughter, and Titus cast daggers at Arsenius, because he courted danger.

"I beg your pardon?" Uncle Titus blushed a vivid red.

"See what you made me do?" Arsenius inquired.

"How is this my fault?" Titus sought shelter but found none.

"You brought it up, when you should have said naught." Then Arsenius lowered his stare. "But you have yet to apprise Uncle Atticus of your mother's revelations."

"What say you?" Father grew quiet, Arsenius waggled his brows, and Titus promised to even the score, at the first opportunity. "You expect me to believe Isobeau was nothing if not pleased with my performance?"

"Actually, Mama said you delayed." Given their newfound camaraderie, in the wake of their talk, Titus could not resist goading his sire. "But it was magic, when *at last* you came together."

"I am not sure how I feel about that, and what did she mean?" Father grimaced, as Uncle Titus chuckled. "In my defense, what would you expect, as we were grieving the loss of my brother, and she was with child. How could I rush her to the marriage bed? And we obviously did something right, as we produced you."

"Let us face it, women are a mystery, and we are but poor souls attempting to navigate their territory." Uncle Titus shifted his weight and grinned. "And what luscious territory it is, which is wherefore we are distracted and often lose our way."

"I second that, as Isobeau has but to flick her fingers, and I am at her service, but do not ever tell her that." Father smiled a smile foreign to Titus, and then his sire snapped to attention. "Which is wherefore you must manage wives with a firm hand."

Arsenius leaned near and said, in a low voice, "This is going to hurt."

"I concur." Oblivious to the secondary discussion, Uncle Titus nodded. "In so many ways, they are like children, in need of direction and discipline, which you must dispense, but never injure them."

"You were the one that told them the truth," Titus whispered. "And I think we should listen to what our mamas recommended, but do us both a favor, and do not admit that to our fathers, or we are in trouble, and I will never make it to the altar."

"Definitely." As their sires extended well-intended but misguided input, about ensuring their wives knew their place and that the men ruled the castle, which could not be more wrong if experience was any indication, Arsenius counted on his fingers. "Bring her flowers, read to her, take her for long rides, just the two of you, talk to her, and listen to her."

"And share her interests." Titus committed the advice to memory, though it sounded more like torture. "But, most important, postpone the consummation, for her sake and your sanity, which I am only too happy to grant."

"Which I did, with much success." Arsenius glanced at their fathers, who argued about various methods of correction for disobedient wives. "Senara kissed me—more than once, and I liked it."

"Oh?" Now that garnered Titus's attention. "Anything interesting happen?"

"To reveal more would be ungentlemanly." Arsenius adopted a cocky stance. "But I am hopeful, cousin."

"*Titus.*" Father stomped a foot on the flagged surface. "Are you listening?"

"Aye, sir." Titus clicked his heels. "Beat her regularly, and keep her with child."

"Uh, Father, I believe it is past due for us to journey to the chapel." Arsenius elbowed Titus in the ribs. "And I should ensure everything is ready for my cousin's nuptials, as he did the same for me."

"Ah, yes." Uncle Titus yanked open the portal. "Come, my son. Let us collect Desi and Senara and away to the chapel."

"I should come with you, as it would not be very wise to keep my fiancée in angst." Titus all but ran toward the door.

"Wait." Father caught Titus by the arm. "I would have words with you, my son."

"Of course." Anxious, he dragged his feet, as he walked toward the hearth and propped an elbow on the mantel. "Is everything all right?"

"There are a few things I would share, on this special occasion." Father eased to one of the two large chairs, near the fire. "Come and sit, as I have long practiced my speech, for this moment, and I would do it justice, although I am nervous."

"You?" Titus settled beside his uncharacteristically tense sire. "Nervous?"

"Aye." Father compressed his lips and gazed at his clenched fists. Then he seemed to relax. "When I married your mother, I did not harbor any great affection for her, but that was not her fault. You see, we were as strangers when I took Isobeau as my wife, in fulfillment of a promise to my brother, and I cannot pretend I knew what I was doing, as the only life I had known was that of a warrior. What is required of a husband is altogether different."

"So I am learning." How Titus wished he had enjoyed such talks with his father, prior to his betrothal. "Have you any real advice to offer?"

"I do, and I hope you are willing to accept the challenge." Father met Titus's stare. "After the wedding, I believed I competed with the memory and the love of my brother. What I later learned was that Isobeau and Titus shared the affection of friends. When we discovered your Uncle Titus was my brother's issue, we realized that Margreit d'Engagne, later Saint-Germain, was Titus's true love. In some respects, that knowledge affirmed the deep and abiding love that your mother and I share. In short, Isobeau owns my heart, but we never would have found love had I not been open to the possibility."

"And you want the same for me." Never had his father spoken with such feeling, and it was not lost on Titus. "You would have me love Rosenwyn."

For as long as he could remember, he admired his father. When he was a boy, he played with a wooden sword and pretended to be the great Lion of the North. Wanted to be like him, in all things. Whereas he once viewed his father as a larger than life knight, they now stood shoulder to shoulder. Yet his father seemed the bigger man, in every way.

"Aye." Father nodded. "It is a provocation unlike any you have ever faced, and it requires bravery, to confront new and unfamiliar territory, sacrifice, to give your heart to another, and trust that Rosenwyn will yield hers to you, and commitment, to nurture and protect that love, as only a man can comprehend, but I submit it is your destiny, as you are a De Wolfe. And should you succeed, the reward is yours for the taking, and it is a priceless treasure, *sans pareil*."

"I hear you, Father." Titus stiffened his spine. "On my honor, I will not disappoint you."

"This is not about me." He sighed. "This is about you achieving the greatest gift of all. But whatever happens, know that I am proud of you."

Just then, Mama flung open the door to the inner bedchamber, and Father stilled and paled. Slowly, he stood, and Titus followed suit. Mama marched directly to Father, perched on her toes, and cupped his cheek.

"You are forgiven for your previous, disingenuous comments, as you have never disciplined me, but that was a lovely speech, and I am sure it soothed your manly pride." Then she kissed him, and Titus averted his stare. "And I love you, too." Just as quick, she stepped back, brushed off the skirt of her emerald green gown, lifted her chin, and snapped her fingers. "Now, let us away, else we will be late for our son's wedding, and that would make me unhappy. I am certain you do not wish to court such danger on what should be an otherwise joyous day."

"We cannot have that, my dear." As she strolled into the hall, Father leaned toward Titus and whispered, "For your own safety, never forget that wives rule the castle."

Titus bit back a snort of laughter. "I know, Father."

PACING BEFORE THE hearth, Rosenwyn wrung her fingers. On the table, a light repast remained untouched, as she was too nervous to eat. At the window, she peered at the ground and pondered an escape, but she suspected she would only succeed in breaking her neck.

"Prithee, do not do it, Rosenwyn." Senara called, as if from afar. "It is not worth it, and we have lost enough."

"In fairness, I was not seriously contemplating a leap." Rosenwyn glanced over her shoulder and smiled at her lifelong friend. "I thought you departed for the chapel."

"I asked my husband if I could ride with you, and he consented, as he is most accommodating." With outstretched arms, Senara drew near, and Rosenwyn walked into her friend's embrace. "In fact, Arsenius is kind, and he extends protection to my family. To my relief, Mama, Papa, and Ysella will remain at Bellesea, and Arsenius promised to secure a suitable match for my sister. Wherefore would he do all that, if he intended to harm me? Is that not wonderful?"

"Of course, and I am happy for you. But what of your union?" She rested her head to Senara's shoulder. "Tell me everything that happened, last night."

"Naught happened." Senara set Rosenwyn at arm's length. "Arsenius suggested we postpone the consummation, until we are better acquainted."

"Indeed?" She opened her mouth and then closed it. "Titus recommended the same delay. What do you make of that?"

"That we are fortunate, because once we take the sacrament, we belong to our husbands, and they have every right to seize what they are owed, with or without our consent." Senara tucked a stray tendril behind her ear. "Given what Mama told me of the deed, and Arsenius's size, I am grateful for the deferment."

"So you know what to expect?" When Senara nodded and blushed, Rosenwyn dragged her friend to the bed, and they sat at the edge of the mattress. "You must share everything you know, as Mama told me naught of the particulars, and I am terrified of the unknown and my future husband."

"You mean you know naught of marital relations?" Senara gasped, when Rosenwyn indicated the affirmative. "Not even what is required of you?"

"I know naught." Given her ignorance, Rosenwyn wanted to cry. "Mama could not bring herself to explain. Will you help me?"

"Oh, dear." Senara clenched her hands. "The information is new to me, and I have yet to put it into practice, but I will share what I know, in Mama's words, which were rather startling, to say the least." She scooted close. "But I cannot say it aloud, as I simply do not possess the nerve or the experience, so I will whisper it in your ear."

"All right. Mayhap it might not prove so shocking." At least, that was what Rosenwyn hoped. However, the more Senara imparted, the more agitated Rosenwyn grew, until she could not sit still. When she could take no more, she pushed from the bed and folded her arms in front of her. "Are you certain that is whither it goes?"

"Aye." Senara dipped her chin. "Believe me, I was just as confused, and I asked Mama to clarify, which she did, much to my distress and embarrassment, but she assured me it will fit."

"I cannot imagine it is possible." In the long mirror, Rosenwyn studied her appearance, and the blue gown, the color of purity, and tried to envision Titus engaging her in the behavior Senara just described, which sounded anything but pure. "While I do not question your mother's honesty, I cannot fathom what you detailed, as it defies reason. Have you ever seen that part of a man? It must be quite small."

"No, and I am in no hurry to, either." Senara bit her lip. "But I know I must yield, as I am Arsenius's wife, and I am just as terrified as you. For our sakes, I hope it is very modest."

A knock at the door brought Rosenwyn alert. "Come."

"We must leave, at once, for the chapel," Petroc replied. "Are you ready?"

"Aye." She remained where she stood. "Senara, I require your assistance, as I do not think I can move."

"You can do it, my friend." Senara offered support. "Just put one foot in front of the other, and it is not so difficult as you might believe."

"I cannot do it." Rosenwyn shook her head. "I cannot marry him. The man is a mountain, and he plans to sleep atop me? He will crush me. As for the rest of the act, absolutely not."

"Do not be silly, and do not be alarmed." Senara

nudged Rosenwyn forward, as Petroc pounded on the wood panel and shouted a second summons. "If you refuse to marry Sir Titus, His Majesty will surely have your head, as well as those of your mother and your brother. You lost your father. Is that not enough?"

"You are right. I know you are right, but that does not make the situation any easier to tolerate." She leaned against her friend and found much needed succor. "But I am tired of being afraid. I need to believe in something. In someone."

"Then take your vows, and be my sister, as well as a De Wolfe." Senara stroked Rosenwyn's plaited hair. "I know you are afraid, because I was, too. But I believe— I have to believe the De Wolfes are honorable people, and you need only have faith."

"Rosenwyn." Petroc again struck the door. "We must go, now."

Resolved to meet the challenge, she stretched upright, wiped a tear, and summoned courage. Clasping her friend's hand, Rosenwyn squared her shoulders and charged forth.

"I apologize, brother, for keeping you waiting." The look on his face gave her pause. "Is something wrong?"

"No, but I feel as though I am delivering you to the

executioner." He bowed his head. "I failed you, Rosenwyn. In father's absence, I did not protect you, but I have a plan that may rescue you both." He glanced at Senara and frowned. "While I cannot delay the nuptials, the fight is just beginning. We may have lost the first battle, but we will win the war."

"Petroc, you must cease such talk, as it would bring about naught but trouble." Senara pulled Rosenwyn past him. "I am married, and you cannot change that. Before God, I pledged my troth, and Arsenius owns me, now."

"You were mine." Petroc snarled as an angry dog. "You were betrothed to me, from birth."

"As subjects of the Crown, we wed by the King's commission." Senara tugged on Rosenwyn's hand, and they descended the stairs. "What we desire must perforce yield to his edicts, on pain of death. We have no choice."

"Mayhap you have surrendered, and I cannot prevent this miscarriage of justice, but that does not mean I am defeated." In the main entry, Petroc took his place at Rosenwyn's side. "I have a plan, and victory will be mine, over the De Wolfes."

"Prithee, lower your voice, or do you wish to destroy us, all?" Glancing left and then right, in search of an unwelcome servant, Rosenwyn wrenched her brother to attention. His argument forced her to accept the terms required of her, and she could not waver in her decision. "What you speak is madness and would bring about naught but misery. Consider Mama, and hold your tongue. I know it wounds your pride, but we must accept that we are the conquered, and I am soon to be the property of Titus de Wolfe. Now, let us away."

With that, she marched into the bailey, to the waiting coach, stepped inside, and eased to the squabs. Senara occupied the place beside Rosenwyn, and Petroc assumed the position opposite the ladies. The equipage lurched forward, and in silence they made the brief but stressful journey to the estate chapel, whither the witnesses gathered.

Tension grew in direction proportion to each successive step that brought her to the altar, as she descended the coach, strolled to the chapel, entered the otherwise charming stone structure, and loomed at one end of the aisle. Filling the pews were the De Wolfes and their extended relations, all of whom smiled and stood, as she approached her husband-to-be.

As Petroc returned to sit beside their mother, Titus drew Rosenwyn near.

"Your hands are cold, my lady." He rubbed her fingers. "And you shiver."

"Apologies, my lord." Garbed all in black, from his doublet to his hose, Titus would have struck terror in the bravest knight, so she considered her reaction understandable. "I am nervous."

"So am I." When he smiled, he revealed a dimple, which did little to dispel his formidable appearance. "What say we rely on each other, to survive?"

"Given the necessary parties are present, let us begin." Vicar Bernard held high the cross. "*In nomine Patris, et Filii, et Spiritus Sancti.*"

The ceremony passed in a haze of fear mixed with nausea, as Rosenwyn swallowed hard and committed herself to a man who remained very much a stranger. To her shame, the vicar had to prompt her more than once for a response, and she cursed herself as her voice shook, but she took her vows, in obeisance of His Majesty's decree. But it was last oath Titus declared, in kind, that persuaded her to reflect on Senara's reasoning.

"From this day forward, you shall not walk alone."

With fingers entwined, Titus met Rosenwyn's stare, and the weight of his gaze seemed to cut through her. "My heart will be your shelter, and my arms will be your home."

"Forasmuch as Sir Titus and Lady Rosenwyn have consented together in holy wedlock, and have witnessed the same before God and this company, and thereto have given and pledged their troth, each to the other, and have declared the same by giving and receiving of a ring, and by joining of hands; I pronounce therefore that they be man and wife, together." Vicar Bernard bade them turn and face the congregation. "*In nomine Patris, et Filii, et Spiritus Sancti*, bless, preserve, and keep you; the Lord mercifully with his favor look upon you; and so fill you with all spiritual benediction and grace, that you may so live together in this life, that in the world to come you may have life everlasting. Amen."

Thus Rosenwyn became Titus's bride.

A cheer reverberated on the stone walls, and the De Wolfes and the De Sheras extended their congratulations, as Titus led Rosenwyn down the aisle and to the coach, which would convey them back to the main residence, whither they would assume a place of honor and partake of a wedding feast.

Yet, she was in no mood to celebrate. As she settled her skirts, her husband draped an arm about her shoulders, and she stiffened her spine.

"Easy, my lady wife." He chuckled. "I wish only to provide warmth, as you appear on the verge of fainting."

"My lord, I am trying to accustom myself to my new station, but there has been little time to adjust." For some reason she could not fathom, she preoccupied herself with his most mysterious part, whither his overgown draped about a peculiar bulge that had previously escaped her notice.

"What are you looking at?" With a finger, he tipped her chin, bringing her gaze to his. "Curious, my dear?" He laughed. "That augurs well for me."

"Nay...that is to say...I only just learned what is demanded of me." She gulped, as the bump swelled in size, beneath her scrutiny. "It does not seem possible."

"Rosenwyn, trust me, when we join our bodies, when we consummate our union, you will enjoy it." To her amazement, he bent his head and pressed his lips to hers, in a gentle affirmation of his reassurance. "And I will never hurt you, so you have no reason to fear me."

Again, he kissed her, but with a little more urgency, and she gasped for air, but he gave her no quarter. In a soft and sweet caress, he brushed his tender flesh to hers, and she found herself reaching for him.

Whither she anticipated fear, she found naught but unshakeable support.

Whither she expected disgust, she experienced naught but fascination—and something else. Something akin to hunger.

And then he retreated.

"Did I do something wrong?" She clutched her throat, as foreign sensations rippled over her, from top to toe.

"No, my dear." He raked his fingers through his hair. "You did everything right, much to my inexpressible pleasure."

"Then why did you stop?" In that moment, she bit her tongue.

"Because if we continued, I would have lifted your ankles, hither." Titus peered at her and grinned. "And our presence is required at the fete in our honor."

"So when do you suppose you will demand what is yours?" Struggling with an unfamiliar ache, she shifted in her seat, as the coach drew to a halt. "When will we seal our vows?"

"Sooner than later, I hope, as we will share a single chamber and a bed, at my insistence." He unlatched the door, jumped to the ground, turned, and lifted her from the equipage. "But when we share our bodies is your decision."

CHAPTER FOUR

SEPTEMBER HERALDED AUTUMN'S arrival with a wicked tempest, marking Titus's first fortnight as the lord of Tharnham Castle. The day after his wedding to Rosenwyn, he departed his childhood home and commenced the long journey, during which he shared a tent and a traveling bed with his spouse, to Truro, in Cornwall, to assume control of the earldom and its stream mining industry. Thus far, he confronted little resistance from the Truronians, who seemed resigned to their position under his rule. Indeed, naught about his new role posed much difficulty or rebellion, with one exception.

His wife.

Whereas the people welcomed his protection, Rosenwyn avoided him at every turn. When he sought her company, she made excuses to avoid him. When they retired, she stacked pillows between them. When she bathed, she barred the door to their quarters. The only time she permitted him the smallest measure of her attention was when he kissed her, every morrow and eventide, and one thing was certain.

She liked his kisses.

And that gave him hope, because his sanity and his patience were wearing thin, and he developed rough spots on his left palm. If he did not claim her soon, he would go mad. So he enacted a plan, on the first sunny day since his arrival, based on his mother's advice on how to court a virgin, and he promised himself to conquer his stubborn bride and her irrational fears.

"The horses are saddled, my lord." Vennor, the steward who proved most loyal in his dealings with Titus, bowed. "And the cook prepared a noon meal, which I bundled with a blanket."

"Perfect." Just then, his beauteous bride appeared, and he admired her brown hair and burgundy, velvet gown. If only he could get beneath her skirts without terrifying her. And he cursed whatever moment of lunacy inspired him to allow her to decide when they consummated their nuptials, because she distracted him to the point that he could not stop thinking about her. "Good morrow, my lady wife."

"My lord." Inclining her head, she smiled. "Vennor

said you wished to see me. Is everything all right? Have I done something wrong?"

"Must you always assume something is wrong, when I summon you?" Ah, she blushed, and his longsword came to attention. "I wish to inspect the tin streaming in the east moorlands, and I want you to accompany me."

"Wherefore?" She blinked, and he could not help but laugh in the face of her confusion.

"Because I desire your company." Titus shifted his weight. "Must I have a reason?"

"Nay, but I am confused." That made two of them. "Would you not prefer Petroc escort you? After all, he is a man."

"Which is wherefore I would not prefer he join me." And her brother made no secret of his disdain for Titus, not that it mattered, because he did not consider Burville a threat. Before Rosenwyn could protest, and she excelled at that, he lifted her to the saddle of a gentle mare. During the brief tenure of their marriage, he discovered his lady coveted an abiding appreciation for horses, and the steward indicated she favored the pastime, thus he intended to indulge her. "I also thought we might ride into Truro, as I have not visited the town, and you promised to grant me a tour of the environs. Do you renege?"

"I would never do that." Her charming pout almost brought him to his knees. "As I am your wife, I am at your service."

"But you will escort me, because you desire my company, too." He tensed. "Do you not?"

"Of course." For some reason, he did not believe her, because he made her nervous. "You are my lord and master."

"First and foremost, I am your husband, and I want to please you." Swift and sure, he gained his mount. "Now, let us away."

When he motioned with his head, Rosenwyn cast a mischievous grin, flicked the reins, and steered the mare to the gate, whither she heeled the flanks, urging the horse into a gallop, and he pursued her into the valley. At the verge, she glanced over her shoulder, as he gave chase, and she pushed harder, as she soared across the heath. While he could have run her aground, he preferred to give her the lead, and she blazed a trail through the Cornish countryside, just as he hoped she would. At a crescent of tall oaks, she slowed the mare to a canter, whither he caught her.

"My lord, that was wonderful." In her excitement, her cheeks flushed a beauteous shade of rose, and she bit her bottom lip. "I should thank you now, in the event I forget to do so, later. It has been so long since I ventured into the moors, and I have missed it. But my father always—"

Silence weighed heavy between them.

"Your father always—what, my dear?" Tears filled her velvety brown eyes, and Titus brought his stallion beside her mare, leaned to the side, and kissed her. "Tell me of him, as I do not want you to feel you cannot mention him in my presence. I did not know your father, and I do not consider him my enemy. Rather, I owe him a debt, as his loss brought me you."

"You would have liked him, and I believe he would have liked you." She sniffed and angled her head, in perfect alignment to receive another kiss, which he offered without delay. "He was an honorable man, beloved by everyone, as he treated our citizens with respect. When he dispensed justice, he did so without bias, and his untimely demise, in defense of our industry, struck our people with inconsolable grief, which was compounded by a cruel twist of fate. Alas, we were not able to remember him and recognize his achievements, properly, as we know not what became of his remains."

"Ah, yes." With a finger, Titus tipped her chin and pressed his lips to hers. "My dear, before we departed Wolflee, I dispatched a missive to London, requesting the return of your father's body, that he might rest in the family crypt."

"What?" Emitting something between a sob and a sigh, Rosenwyn reached for him, which startled the mare. As she toppled, he lunged, caught her beneath the arms, and pulled her into his lap. "Oh, you sweet, beauteous man."

As she showered his face in kisses, Titus de Wolfe, warrior knight, servant of the Crown, son of the great Lion of the North, and descendant of William de Wolfe, just sat there and grinned. When she stretched the limits of his self-control, he ended the tempting tryst.

"Am I to presume I made you happy?" Cradling her head, he pulled his cloak about her, when a gust of wind buffeted them. "Because I want to please you, my lady."

"Wherefore?" The pain in her expression brought him low. "I am the defeated. I am property. My happiness is of no account."

"That is not true, and you are not property. You are my wife." As his father's counsel echoed in his ears, Titus nudged her nose with his and stole another kiss. "In so many ways, you are my greatest strength, and I admire your spirit. With your permission, I would rely on your knowledge and include you in many aspects of the estate duties, which you already maintain, unless you prefer to surrender your responsibilities."

"Oh, no." As he expected, she perched upright, her excitement evident. "While I will relinquish whatever you ask, I would be of use, as I know everyone. And I understand the miners, because I often accompanied my father, so I can provide information when you negotiate with the workers. After all, I am a Burville."

"But you were born to be a De Wolfe." With care, he returned her to the mare. "Shall we continue?"

"Aye, my lord." When she gave her attention to the road, he studied her elegant features and realized he never wanted any woman more than he wanted Rosenwyn, though he knew not wherefore he found her so appealing. Even when the local whores plied their wares, they inspired naught but disgust, as he desired none but Rosenwyn. Was she not the same as any other lady?

Of course, not.

She was his wife, to protect and defend, as only a husband could guard her. As Papa stated, Rosenwyn manifested the supreme challenge, and her heart was the greatest reward. As a De Wolfe, pride demanded he seize her. As a man, he had to have her. Thus, he would conquer her, and in so doing they would both win.

"What is the overseer's name?" At a rise, he drew rein and surveyed the tin streaming operation, in the valley below. "And how long has he worked for your family?"

"He is called Credan, and he has been in the employ of the Burvilles since before I was born, as was his father, before him." She guided Titus down to the impressive operation, which utilized a maze of wooden ramps to divert water and separate the sand and silt from the heavier tin. "My lord, although we are vanquished, Truronians are proud men. I would have you consider that, when you address them."

"Wise counsel, my beauteous bride." He winked, and she giggled. "Shall we make our approach, and I will follow you?"

"I suggest we ride past, as they are about their

tasks." His lady handled the mare as an expert, and he envied the grace with which she managed the downhill stretch. "Papa always conferred with Credan, in brief, to ensure all needs were met but did not disturb them too long."

"Then I shall do the same, my dear." Drawing his stallion to a halt, Titus waved to the overseer. "Good morrow, Credan. And how are you?"

"Lord Vael." Credan bowed and snapped his fingers, and the miners ceased their labors. "How may I be of service?"

"Actually, hither I have traveled to offer my services." Titus acknowledged various miners, who stopped to greet the new earl and his bride. While he genuinely enjoyed Rosenwyn's company, he had another reason for asking her to accompany him, and that was to reassure her people that she was well treated. "Lady Vael informs me that the previous Lord Vael relied on you to manage the stream mining."

"Indeed, my lord." Credan nodded. "If you wish to alter the arrangement, I will not protest."

"But I would protest." Titus chuckled, in hopes of dispelling any tension, as the workers gathered near, because he wanted to make a good impression. "Unless you have need of me, I rely on your expertise in the industry, to ensure we produce enough tin to fulfill our obligations. In regard to the business, I have no plans to change anything, without your recommendation."

"So I am to maintain my position?" Credan raised his voice when he spoke, as though he alerted the miners. "Naught will change?"

"Only by your authority." A chorus of murmurs circulated through the miners, and Titus smiled at the overseer. "And if there is anything else you require, you have only to ask."

"Gramercy, my lord." Credan shuffled his feet. "I had thought of increasing our yield, by mining copper and clay, if your lordship is amenable. Given the outcome at Blackheath, numerous men have need of work, and the additional ores could provide more income for the estate."

"That is a wise proposition." Titus noted the relief in countless faces. "Come to dinner, Thursday next, at Tharnham, and we will discuss how to move forward with your plan."

"I will do so, Lord Vael, and I look forward to it." Again, Credan bowed and then gave his attention to Rosenwyn. "Lady Vael, on behalf of the men, allow me to congratulate you on your wedding."

"Gramercy, Credan." She turned the mare to face the crowd. "It is good to be home, and I am fortunate that His Majesty has seen fit to bless me with a kind and generous husband. Indeed, his lordship petitioned the Crown, that we might receive my father's remains and honor him, properly."

Another series of hushed undertones circulated through the miners, but they quieted, when Credan splayed an upraised palm, and Titus availed himself of his bride's influence. As she talked to the miners, he realized his bride was a skillful negotiator, and he would do well to employ her abilities, in future dealings with the miners.

"May I inquire after your mother, the former Lady Vael?" the overseer inquired, with a half smile.

"Mama is well, but she misses my father." Rosenwyn averted her stare. "Whether or not my father's body is returned to us, we will arrange a ceremony, and you will all be invited to pay respects."

In that moment, Credan stared at Titus, as if assessing his reaction.

"I shall ask the vicar to dedicate a service and designate an official period of mourning." Titus shifted in the saddle. "And we will celebrate the late Lord Vael's life and achievements, with a feast at Tharnham."

"We will be there, my lord," a young miner replied.

"Then we should away, as Lady Vael promised to escort me about Truro." Titus turned his destrier, and his wife followed in his wake. As the miners bade farewell, he steered toward the village. "That was inspiring, my lady wife."

"Husband, I could not agree more, and the feast is a lovely idea." She pulled alongside, as he slowed his stallion. "If I may, will you bathe prior to dining, this eventide?"

"I will." That question caught him unaware, but did not altogether surprise him, as she always avoided their chamber when he tended himself, and he met her gaze, anticipating trepidation. What he spied remained rather unfamiliar. "Wherefore do you ask?"

"If you wait until after I check with the cook, re-garding the meal, I will wash your back." In the sunshine, she glowed, and his heart pounded in his chest, as it was the first time she expressed an interest in fostering intimacy. "It is my duty, is it not?"

A SENNIGHT PASSED since Rosenwyn assumed a particular marital responsibility, and still she could not bring herself to consummate her vows. As she stood at the table in the kitchen, cutting a root to season the cameline sauce for brewets, Titus's favorite dish, in preparation for the feast to welcome the miners, she revisited the sweet kisses they shared, the previous eventide, as she washed his impressive chest. What she did not anticipate was the effects of her tender ministrations, because she possessed no real knowledge of the male form.

After a few moments of bliss, wherein she feared she might swoon, given the assault on her senses whenever their lips met, he drew her hand to that part of his body that fascinated her, and one touch of her fingers to his most bellicose protuberance inspired a strong reaction. When she assumed she broke something of importance, he explained, much to his obvious mortification, that his was but an inadvertent emission, proof of his uncontrollable desire for her.

"Jenifry, whither is the firkin of Lord Vael's ale?" Rosenwyn composed a list of items with which to treat her husband, that eventide, as she wished to make amends for his embarrassment. While she regretted causing his distress, the power she wielded posed an irresistible lure, and she longed to know more, yet she delayed the consummation. Endeavoring to show her husband that she appreciated him, she resolved to pick the perfect moment to seal their vows. "And we should make some of the herbed bread he prefers."

"Aye, my lady." The scullery maid narrowed her stare. "And the ale is in the undercroft, near the wine."

"Then I should fetch the firkin." Drying her hands on her apron, Rosenwyn turned and navigated the narrow passage that led to the stores beneath the castle. As she neared, she noted a heated discussion. "Hello? Who is there?"

"Shh." Petroc stood and quieted a small group of his friends. "What do you want, Rosenwyn?"

"I am in search of Titus's ale. What are you doing?" The three young men rushed past her, as she approached. "Wherefore do you gather, hither? What mischief are you about?"

"Naught that concerns you." As Petroc tried to evade her, she grabbed his arm, and he wrenched free. "Mind your own affairs, as you seem quite content with that *De Wolfe*."

"This may surprise you, brother, but that name is

no insult, and I can only hope to do it credit." In disgust, she straightened his tunic and ran her fingers through his unruly hair. "Look at you, dressed like a servant when we expect guests. Have you no pride? Are you so consumed with unfounded anger that you forget what it means to be a Burville? Have you no respect for Mama or for Papa's memory?"

"I would ask the same of you, sister." He spat. "You take to De Wolfe's bed as a common whore, bartering our heritage to a murderous cur."

"Cease your mindless complaints, as I grow weary of your insanity." At her wit's end, she gritted her teeth and prayed for calm. "And I am no whore. I am his wife, legally bound by the sacrament."

"And how easy you surrendered." He sneered. "Our father does not rest in our crypt, and you fret over food and drink for the man who may have killed our sire."

"You know, very well, that reports of the battle contend that Papa fell to Suffolk's men, while Titus fought for Lord Daubeney." Frustrated, Rosenwyn stomped a foot. "Must you continue a fight that has long since ended? Has there not been enough bloodshed to satisfy your thirst for revenge against a man whose only crime is that he obeyed the King's command? Our father, God rest him, along with the other Cornish rebels, flouted the Crown's authority, when they marched on London, and my husband harbors no ill will. While I would assert our cause was just, that gave us no right to attack His Majesty, yet Titus has no quarrel with us. Wherefore must you agitate him, when we are defeated, yet he treats us as equals?"

"I will never cede the war." Squaring his shoulders, Petroc rested fists on hips. "I will kill De Wolfe and avenge our father's death."

"Are you mad?" In shock, she clutched her throat. "Do you not realize that a threat against my husband is a threat to me? Do you not fathom the impossibility of my situation? Would you put me between you? I beg you, do not force me to choose between loyalty to my husband and love for you, because you will lose. I must believe that yours are the misguided words of an irrational man driven by unutterable hatred, and that is not the brother I know and love. Prithee, you must stop your campaign of terror against Titus, as I fear the consequences, should you continue to conspire against him."

"All right, sister." Her brother inclined his head

and smiled a smile she did not trust, for an instant. "I will do my best to mend ways with De Wolfe." Then he glanced at the firkin. "What do you want with ale, when you prefer wine?"

"It is Titus's favorite, and I would serve it at the feast." When she reached for the small cask, Petroc brushed her aside.

"Allow me." To her relief, he lifted the firkin. "Whither do you want it?"

"Prithee, in the kitchen." As she followed him, retracing her earlier steps, she studied his posture, as he appeared to relax. "Then I would have you make yourself ready, as I would present a united front, De Wolfe and Burville, together, when our guests arrive."

"Of course." Petroc set the firkin on the table and then faced her. "As you said, we must honor Papa's memory, and I live for that singular purpose."

"I am so glad to hear it." With that, she pressed a chaste kiss to her brother's cheek.

"My lady." Vennor bowed. "A messenger is just arrived, with a letter for you."

"Oh?" She accepted the envelope and noted the seal. "How curious."

"Will that be all, sister?" Petroc loomed at attention.

"Aye, my dear brother." She waved and opened the missive. "I will see you in the receiving line." To the cook, Rosenwyn said, "I should dress for the feast, and do not forget the pastries with jelly, as I promised them to Lord Vael, especially."

"Aye, my lady." The cook nodded once. "Everything will be as you directed."

As she strolled into the screened corridor at the rear of the great hall, she unfolded the parchment, scanned the contents, and halted. Then she slowly read the note.

My dearest Rosenwyn,

It pains me to inform you of a dreadful tiding, but I must warn you of dangerous double-dealings, involving Petroc. To my heartfelt remorse, your brother threatens the lives of our husbands, and I have failed in my attempts to dissuade him from his perilous path, which forebodes naught but misery. While I have not shared the distressing revelations with Arsenius, it is only a matter of time before I must do so, as I have grown to care for my husband, and I cannot deceive him. Thus, I feel compelled to inform you of these sad developments, that you might act to divert what could be disastrous for our families.

In love and sisterhood,
Senara

Rosenwyn's fingers trembled, as she held tight to the dispatch. In the great hall, servants arranged the tables and hung banners in the Vael colors, festooned with the signature wolf's head sigil, which Titus commissioned for the event, to represent the marriage of two great legacies. It was a thoughtful touch and one that was not lost on her. In the furthermost corner, a group of musicians sounded various notes.

As she stumbled forward, she shoved the letter into the fitchet of her cotehardie and hugged herself. Overcome with emotion, at the prospect of losing her husband, she discovered she was not so immune to his attentions, as she once presumed. Indeed, she harbored a measure of affection for him.

Driven by the need to defend her man, she ran into the entry, whither the steward issued orders to the staff. When Vennor spotted her, he faced her.

"My lady." The steward stretched tall. "I instructed the master of the horse to organize the coaches and horses at the south end of the bailey, to reduce the crowds at the main doors."

"Excellent." She swallowed hard. "Whither is Lord Vael?"

"He retired to the solar, to dress for the feast," Vennor replied. "May I be of service?"

"Gramercy, but I should follow Lord Vael's example." She forced a smile. "We shall return, momentarily."

Holding high her chin, she walked to the steps and ascended to the second level, whither she shared the master's chambers with her husband. By the time she reached the solar, she ached to hold Titus.

In their inner suite, she found him, resplendent in his doublet and hose of black, which he paired with an overgown of deep blue, trimmed in gold, and she marched straight to him. Without a word, she slipped her arms about his waist and rested her head to his chest.

"Good eventide, my beauteous bride." As usual, he enfolded her in his supportive embrace, and she sighed. "Are you all right?"

"I am, now." Relaxing, she hummed, as he kneaded her back, along her spine. "You will remain close to me, this eventide."

"Of course." He shuffled her in his grasp. "What is wrong, Rosenwyn? Wherefore are you afraid?"

"My lord, you mistake nervousness for fear." She lied, and it cut through her like the sharpest sword. "This is our first formal appearance, and this is my coming out, as Lady Vael. I would make you proud."

"My dear, I could never be anything less." As was his way, he patted her bottom. "Now, you should dress for the event, as we do not want to be late. Shall I summon your maid?"

"Nay, my lord." Holding his stare, she savored newfound confidence. "Rather, I would have you assist me."

Blushing, he opened his mouth and closed it, and she laughed.

"Are you sure?" He furrowed his brow and shuffled his feet. "Because I have always imagined undressing you."

"But you are more than able, my beauteous husband." From a small side chamber, she retrieved the garment she made for the feast, and she hoped he would note the significance of the colors. When she returned, she gave him her back. "Will you untie my laces?"

"Your wish is my command." He cleared his throat, when she doffed her gown. "But I think you are trying to drive me mad, as I would lock you hither, until the morrow."

"Oh?" She pulled the new frock over her head. "And what would we do, to pass the time, my lord?"

"Given my promise, that would be up to you." Ah, he was naught if not faithful to his word, as he tied her laces. "But I long to make love to you, Rosenwyn."

It was the first time he ever declared such.

"Titus." She uttered his name as a whisper of a summons and then faced him.

While she expected a series of fervent kisses, her husband just stood there and stared.

"You wear the De Wolfe black and gold." Then he traced the telltale design she embroidered over her heart. "And you bear the wolf's head."

"For all to know that I am a De Wolfe." She cupped his cheek. "And I am yours."

"Rosenwyn." A mountain of aroused male pounced on her, and she loved every bit of it.

As their lips met, and tongues twined, something undeniable and fierce blossomed between them, and she savored the unquenchable hunger and unyielding devotion not even her brother could diminish. Breathing heavily, Titus ended their all too brief tryst, much to her chagrin.

"Sweetheart, if we continue, I am going to make a mess of my braies, and then we will be late for the feast." He claimed another quick kiss. "And I would escort my wife, for everyone to see, as I am but a humble beggar at your side."

For a moment, she reflected on Petroc's hateful declaration, and she mulled whether or not to share the words with Titus. But how would he react to the news? Settling her palm in the crook of his elbow, she turned toward the door. "Then let us away, my lord."

CHAPTER FIVE

A COMMOTION AT the gate brought Titus to attention, as he inventoried the goods he purchased in Truro, to see them through the winter months. The master of the horse rushed from the stable, to greet their visitors, as a wagon, accompanied by the king's escort, as proclaimed by the royal standard, steered toward the main residence, and he turned to the merchant.

"Gramercy, good sirrah. Everything is as I ordered." Titus handed the merchant an envelope. "Hither are instructions, to be delivered to the goldsmith. The item is to be fashioned to my exact requirements, at the agreed upon price."

After the successful feast, to foster amity with the miners, Titus negotiated, with his wife's assistance, new contracts to begin stream mining copper and clay, in exchange for increased wages, to the benefit of all parties, ushering in a new period of prosperity for the earldom. To show his appreciation of Rosenwyn's efforts, he decided to observe a long-standing De Wolfe custom, and he hoped his gift might encourage her to take the last step and consummate their vows, before he ran wild for want of her.

And how he desired her.

"Aye, Lord Vael." The merchant nodded. "I am your servant."

"Lord Vael." The King's soldier neared, came to a halt, bowed, and handed Titus a rolled parchment. "I am Sir Galeren Fruhwirth, of His Majesty's guard. By the Crown's command, and observing all proprieties, I return the remains of Cador Burville, the late Lord Vael, thereby fulfilling my commission."

"Welcome, Sir Fruhwirth. I am in your debt, and I invite you to break your journey, hither, and enjoy a night at Tharnham Castle, as honored guests." Titus signaled Vennor and said to the steward, "See to it that the King's men are properly sheltered and fed, and send for Vicar Lievremont, at once. Also, whither is Lady Vael?"

"Aye, my lord, and Lady Vael was in the kitchen when last I saw her." Vennor snapped his fingers and issued directives.

It was then Titus noted the growing crowd, as word spread of the arrivals. Before he could dispatch a warning to his wife, as he would temper the shock, she ran into the bailey, and he leaped into her path.

"Rosenwyn, wait." With an arm about her waist, he lifted her into his embrace, as the coffret, decorated with carved ivory, featuring warriors and dancers, and a latch and hinges of gold, in an unmistakable demonstration of esteem, was lowered from the wagon. "Sweetheart, you should let the vicar bless the remains."

"I do not understand." She craned her neck. "Wherefore is the box so small, when my father was a man of large stature?"

"What did they do to him?" With a mighty scowl, Petroc, the bane of Titus's existence, along with Rosenwyn's mother, Lady Endelyn, pushed past Titus. "What further humiliation does the King inflict on our father?"

"Petroc—*no*," Titus shouted.

In that moment, to Titus's horror, Petroc flipped the latch and opened the coffret, revealing the cleaned bones, therein. Before a soldier could close the lid, Lady Endelyn screamed and fainted, and Rosenwyn sobbed.

"Petroc, for the love of all that is holy, help your mother." Titus held tight to his bride, as she burst into tears. "Easy, my lady wife." To the steward, he said, "Vennor, have the coffret taken to the chapel, whither Lord Vael may lay in state, until such time as we can arrange a funeral service and receive those citizens who would make their obedience."

"Aye, sir." Vennor clapped once, and soldiers from the garrison retrieved the coffret.

"Wherefore should you treat my father with respect when the King has already violated the body?" Petroc bared his teeth, and Titus prayed for patience. "You smile to my face, but you spit on my heritage, De Wolfe dog. You did this—admit it."

"Have care how you speak to me, boy." At the end of his tether, and struggling to contain Rosenwyn, Titus lowered his chin and cast a lethal stare. "I grow weary of your caustic remarks, which I would address, but now is neither the time nor the place to fight that battle."

"Do not lecture me, De Wolfe, as I have no need of your counsel." Petroc ignored his unconscious mother, as she collapsed on the ground, and he shook his fist.

"But you will pay for your insult to my father."

"*Vennor.*" Ignoring the Burville gadling, Titus called to the steward. "See that Lady Endelyn is carried to her chamber, and have the physic assess her condition."

With that, Titus patted Rosenwyn's back, as she rested her head to his shoulder and wept, and he conveyed her to the solar. When he tried to put her down, she refused to let go, so he shuffled her in his arms and sat at one of the chairs they often occupied, as they discussed plans for the stream mines, at eventide.

"Rosenwyn, prithee, do not cry, as I can bear anything but your tears." While he regretted her distress, there was something powerful in the knowledge that when she needed comfort, she sought it in his embrace. "Come, love. Your father has been gone since June, and you were happy that I petitioned His Majesty for the remains. Wherefore do you cry?"

"Did you not see the condition of my father's body?" Shifting, she met his gaze, and his gut wrenched, given her misery. "Wherefore would the King torture my father? Was it not enough that we were defeated?"

"Torture?" Titus blinked. "My lady, you have thoroughly confused me. How did His Majesty torture your father's remains?"

"My lord, did you not see?" She sobbed anew. "He is naught but bones."

"Aye." He tried but failed to discern the source of her discomfit. "That is customary."

"Customary?" Now Rosenwyn blinked. "How so?"

"Sweetheart, I suspect that when your father fell, on the field of glory, his body was collected, to be boiled in either Adam's ale or wine."

"What?" She shrieked. "How horrible."

"Nay, my dear, it is neither horrible nor abusive, and you weep for naught." With his thumbs, he wiped her cheeks. "The flesh rots soon after death, and such decay is considered offensive to the memory of the dead, thus it is separated from the bones and buried. It is a process known as *mos Teutonicus*, afforded to only the bravest soldiers, and it is done in a show of respect, to honor those of noble blood. Believe me, His Majesty's intent is right and true."

"I have never heard of such a thing." She sniffed, rested against his chest, and sighed. "But then I have no previous experience with war, so I must rely on your expertise. However, it was rather disturbing to witness."

"I know, my dear." He nuzzled her forehead and savored the steady beat of her heart. Rubbing her shoulder, he tipped her chin and claimed a kiss. "Should I fall in the heat of conflict, far from Tharn-ham, my remains would be similarly treated, that they might be returned to you, with deference, and I would have it no other way."

"Oh, I cannot fathom that." To his infinite grati-tude, she hugged him. "You must promise never to leave me."

"Sweet wife, were the choice mine, I would never abandon your company." With a finger, he traced the curve of her ear. "But I am the King's servant, and I must go whither I am sent, yet I vow that I shall take only that which is required to defend the Crown, while the best part of me will always reside in your cherished embrace."

"Am I so special, to merit such assurances?" It dawned on him then that she had no idea that she meant more to him than she realized. "We have yet to seal our vows, in the most intimate deed."

"Owing to my pledge, the date of that joyous occasion is yours to fix, but I submit that what we share exceeds the bonds of a physical union." Thus Titus stood at the banks of his Rubicon, and his next statement could determine the fate of his fledgling marriage. Taking a moment to compose himself, he distracted her with a few delicious kisses. When he broke their connection, he pulled her exceedingly near, as to render the distinctions between them indiscernible. "Is it possible my devotion has escaped your notice? If so, then I failed in my duty as your husband, and I should remedy that oversight." Meeting her stare, he swallowed hard and threw down the gauntlet. "Rosenwyn, I care for you."

With something between a sob and a sigh, she advanced on his person, and never had he savored such a delectable, if a tad disorganized, invasion. Surrendering to her adorable if less than elegant attempts at seduction, he honored his promise and permitted her to dictate the course of their tryst, and how she captured him.

"Oh, Titus." She pressed her soft and feminine form to him, and he almost let fly his seed in his braies, as he held his breath in anticipation of her admission. "I would have you know that I—"

A knock intruded on their love play, and he cursed.

"Who is it?" he barked, as his bride pushed from his lap and wiped her brow. "And wherefore do you intrude on our privacy?"

"I beg your pardon, but Lady Endelyn requests the presence of Lady Vael." A maid entered the chamber and bowed her head. "My lord, the physic cannot calm Lady Endelyn, and he believes only Lady Vael can soothe Lady Endelyn's agitation."

The same could be said of Titus.

"Of course." Rosenwyn dried her face. "My lord, I should tend my mother."

"Aye, my lady." As she departed, Titus admired the gentle sway of her hips and considered the fact that she did not return his declaration. Then again, they had not made love. Alone in the quiet of their chamber, it struck him as altogether diverting that his father's words rang true.

Indeed, a woman's heart manifested a treasure, *sans pareil*. Thus the battle-hardened warrior faced his most challenging conquest. But a De Wolfe would never be deterred, and never would he falter, so he would woo his wife. Somehow, some way, Titus vowed that one day, he would win his resistant lady's heart.

LIFE RETURNED TO its usual routine, in the fortnight after the period of mourning Titus designated to honor Rosenwyn's father. As the estate thrived, and she settled into her duties as Lady Vael, she decided it was time to become a De Wolfe bride, irrevocably.

And that required a consummation.

Whereas the mere thought once made her violently ill, now she experienced naught but a shiver of excitement, because her thoughtful husband promised naught but pleasure in the act, and she trusted him.

But how to convey her desires without embarrassing herself?

As she mulled the prospects, she walked straight into Petroc.

"Oh, brother." She almost toppled, but he grabbed her none too gently by the arms and held her upright. "Apologies, as I was distracted."

"No doubt, by the De Wolfe dog." He glared, and anger welled in the pit of her belly. "But I shall exact recompense for our slights, even if you and Mama have surrendered the fight."

"What fight?" Frustrated by his continued combative nature, she splayed her palms. "Are you not tired of resisting all that Titus offers us? He revered Papa, he treats Mama with respect and kindness, he is devoted to me, and he supports you, despite your constant complaints, yet you do naught but agitate and threaten him. Do you honestly believe you could best him, in battle, given his stature and prowess, which is indisputable?"

"Then I shall die as a warrior." The scourge waved a clenched fist, and she wanted to scream. "But I submit mine is the greater cause, and I will kill the cur and restore our legacy to—"

In that instant, she slapped him. "You shall die a fool, and you will go to your grave, as a nameless sack of embarrassment, to be forgotten."

"Wherefore do you take his side against me, your own blood?" Rubbing his cheek, which bore the imprint of her hand, he retreated. "Are you not a Burville?"

"I am a De Wolfe, bound by my oath and the sacrament, and you would do well to remember that." Clenching her jaw, she checked her tone, as a servant lingered in the hall. "As I once told you, a threat against my husband is a threat against me, and I will defend him, with my life, if necessary. If you cannot forget the sorrowful events of the past, which were not of our making, then you will leave this castle and make your own way. But you will go in peace, or you will deal with me, and you may not like the consequences."

"Then I take your leave, *my lady.*" To her regret, Petroc bowed, with an exaggerated flourish, no doubt intended to mock her. "And I wish you naught but misery in your capitulation, that you might suffer the consequences of your betrayal."

"Get out." She shoved him hard. "Be gone from my sight, that you might burden me, no more. And I shall make your excuses to Mama, though I suppose you will not be missed."

"I am going, sister." He smirked, and the hair at her nape stood on end. "But I have friends, and I will have my revenge. I will not rest until that cursed dog is in the ground, that I might spit upon his remains."

Tears welled, as Petroc turned on a heel and ran down the corridor. As children, he was her champion, and his departure tore at her gut. Yet, what most disconcerted her was the danger he posed to her husband.

Driven by the need to protect Titus, to hold him

safely in her unyielding embrace, she returned to the solar. What awaited her brought her to a halt.

"Good eventide, my beauteous bride." Standing at the table, and garbed in one of his finest tunics and overgowns, in the De Wolfe black and gold, Titus lifted the lid on a covered dish, to reveal her favorite meal of savory pourcelet farci. "Since we shelter no guests, and all is quiet, I thought we could sup in the privacy of our chambers, and you can take the meal as you sit in my lap, because I would feed you."

"Titus." With the flick of her wrist, she slammed shut the door and then rushed into his outstretched arms. With Petroc's horrible accounts echoing in her ears, she hugged her husband about the waist and vowed never to let go. "You spoil me, so. What have I done to deserve such gifts?"

"You have exceeded my requirements, in every way, and thanks to your assistance, the mines yield heretofore unheard of profits." He kissed the top of her plaited hair. "Wherefore do you weep, when I wanted only to please you?"

"It is just that I am so happy." And she needed to be near him, to remind herself that he was hale and whole. "But I should wipe my face, else I shall ruin your lovely gesture."

"Are you sure you are all right?" Frowning, he released her. "You shiver, my dear. Is something wrong?"

"My lord, everything is wonderful. Now, let us enjoy the fruits of your labors, that I might show my appreciation, in a manner I hope will satisfy you, anon." That garnered a wink and a smile, as he plopped to the bench, and she rolled her shoulders, as she lifted the pitcher of ale and filled his goblet. As he prepared to take a drink, she detected a strange odor, sniffed the contents of the ewer, and knocked the goblet from his grasp. "*No.*"

"Wherefore did you do that?" He cast an expression of confusion.

"It is poison." She reflected on Petroc's thirst for revenge and realized she needed to tell Titus everything, as she passed him the pitcher. "Bitter almonds."

"God's bones." He followed her example and came alert. "This was no accident. Someone tried to kill me."

"No, it was not, and you are correct in your assertion." She shook her head, as something inside her fractured. "And I suspect I know who did it."

"What?" Slowly, he stood and leveled his stare on

her, and she shrank beneath the weight of his scrutiny. "Who would do such a cowardly thing?"

"Petroc." And it killed her to admit it. Determined to leave naught hidden, Rosenwyn collected Senara's letter, from the small chest, whither she concealed it. In the solar, she gave the missive into Titus's hands. Then she recounted the various exchanges, including the heated discussion in the undercroft. "He has made numerous threats against you, and I turned him out of the house, ere I came to you, this eventide."

"And when were you going to inform me of the sad developments?" Something in Titus's demeanor gave her pause, as he narrowed his glare. "Wherefore did you not warn me, that I might be on guard?"

"I feared you might kill my brother." The hurt in his countenance struck her as a blow to the face, and she flinched. "But I know you would never hurt my kin. Yet, I would remind you that we were strangers when first we met and married. In truth, you were the enemy, and I was but your reward. I knew not how you would react to Petroc's foolish campaign against you, so I protected him, hoping I could reason with him. Alas, I was mistaken."

"Do you think so little of me?" he inquired, in a low

voice.

"Nay, my lord." Abandoning any measure of self-preservation, she flung herself at her knight. "Since our wedding ceremony, I have learned through your actions, which lend much to your credit, that you are the best of men, and I am a fortunate wife."

"Pretty words, from one who keeps secrets from me." He tried to put her aside, but she refused to relinquish her hold. Instead, she pressed herself to him, in the manner that always garnered a pleasurable response. "What are you doing?"

"Prithee, Titus, do not deny me, as I long for your comforting embrace." When she tried to kiss him, he turned away, so she pressed her lips to his neck. "But I would be more, if you let me. I would be yours. I would seal our vows, forever securing our union, so that naught and no one could ever take you from me."

"Do you propose to dissuade me from confronting Petroc, by at last yielding your bride's prize? Do you believe yourself irresistible, that I should be deterred from my proper course?" Clutching her shoulders, he shook her twice, and she whimpered. "I come to you honestly, with naught but honorable intentions, and you would defile our marriage bed in a pitiful attempt to sway me? Trust me, my lady wife, I am not so desperate as you believe, and what lies between your legs is as much the same as any other quim, which I caution you not to use as a weapon against me, because you will fail."

"And never would I do anything so heinous, because I care for you, too, so I will forgive your slight." Reaching behind her, she tugged at her laces and ripped her gown, but she concerned herself not with modesty, as she dropped the velvet to the floor. After kicking off her slippers, she squared her shoulders, determined to surrender her most intimate flesh, not as a sacrifice, but as an expression of unimpeachable fealty. Covered in naught but her chemise, she met her resistant husband. "What I offer is not some sort of gift, to be bartered as a means to an end. Rather, it is a symbol of unwavering loyalty, which I pledge to you, and you alone, if you will accept me. Whatever you decide, you may do with me as you wish, as I am your humble servant, and I would give my life for you, which I made clear to my brother, before I cast him from our home."

Quiet fell on the solar, and she did not falter.

Without hesitation or shame, she untied the ribbon

of her chemise and shrugged free of the fine garment. In silence, she promised to endure his choice, with the grace and ease expected of a De Wolfe bride. To her surprise, Titus uttered naught but her name, a bare whisper, as he knelt at her feet and kissed her belly.

CHAPTER SIX

S UNLIGHT FILTERED THROUGH the lancet windows, casting a mosaic across the floor, as Titus admired his sleeping wife. Heaven on earth rested between the sheets, as she smiled a feminine smile, and he could only guess the subject of her dreams, but he expended considerable effort to ensure she remained abed, as he had an errand of importance to complete, and he hoped to find her still in blissful slumber, upon his return.

After skulking quietly across the solar, he opened the door, slipped into the hallway, shut the heavy wood panel, and exhaled. Whistling a frisky little tune, he descended the stairs, two at a time, and charged into the bailey, whither he flagged the steward.

"Vennor, send for the master of the horse, and have my stallion saddled." Smiling, Titus pulled on his gloves and shifted his weight. A series of breathy sighs and hushed whispers of devotion filled his ears, as he recalled his bride's sweet surrender, and his longsword prepared for battle, but he tamped his hunger, as he would not abuse Rosenwyn's delicate flesh. To his supreme satisfaction, he had at last conquered his prey, and hers was a most precious yield. "And ensure Lady Vael is not disturbed, but if she wakes, have her maid ready a hot bath, and have the cook prepare a substantial meal. Tell my lady that I have journeyed to Truro, on an urgent commission, and I must speak with Credan, and then I shall return."

"Aye, sir." The steward frowned. "Will you not take a compliment of soldiers with you?"

"Nay, as I will not be gone long, and neither do I travel far." Just then, the master of the horse appeared, and Titus strolled to his destrier. Considering Petroc's threats, which his wife recited, in detail, he paused. "But I would take my swords, if you will retrieve them."

"Right away, my lord." Vennor clapped twice and a gadling ran toward the garrison, whither Titus stored his armor and weapons.

As Titus mounted his destrier, he grimaced, because his fire-breathing dragon ached to invade Rosenwyn's tender territory, and he resolved to take the long route into the village, to cool his blood.

"By your command, my lord." Vennor handed Titus the unique curved blades.

After securing his pair of Damascus swords, he heeled the flanks of his destrier and galloped past the gates. A brisk wind thrummed through his hair, and he inhaled the fresh air. Just as quick, cherished visions of Rosenwyn filled his senses, as he revisited the moment he claimed her.

Despite his experience, never had he known a woman could blush from head to toe, and he chuckled as he reflected on her gaze of unmistakable wonder, when he joined their bodies. But it was the memory of her healthy scream, which he would wager rattled the curtain wall about Tharnham, and with which she heralded her virgin release, that he would carry into the hereafter. And it did much to soothe his injured pride, after their first argument.

Indeed, she seemed intent on proving the depth of her desire, as she made love to him into the dawn hours. It was in the relative solitude of his outing that he realized he had fallen in love with his wife, and no one could have been more surprised.

Anxious to return to Rosenwyn, he decided to

collect the expensive gift and postpone the meeting with Credan, as he wondered how his wife would express her appreciation of his generosity.

In the environs of Truro, he navigated the maze of narrow streets, until he arrived at the goldsmith's place of business. At the door, he knocked and then entered.

"Hello?" Surveying the inventory of treasures, Titus doffed his gloves. "Hammett, are you there?"

"Lord Vael." The goldsmith wiped his hands on his leather apron. "I have been expecting you." From a shelf, he drew a box covered in black velvet. "The item is ready, as you requested. If you will have a seat, you may inspect the bracelet."

At a table, Titus pulled out a chair and took his ease. When the goldsmith lifted the lid, Titus swelled with pride. From a bed of cotton, he gently picked up the fine-wrought chain, from which a wolf's head pendant, an exact likeness of the sigil that adorned every De Wolfe knight's ailette, dangled. It was a longstanding tradition, dating to the time of William De Wolfe, to gift a De Wolfe bride with the bracelet.

"It is masterful craftsmanship, Hammett." Slowly, Titus laid the bracelet atop the cotton. "I shall pay you double the agreed price, in copper ore." Then he glanced at another bauble. "And what do you want for the circlet, with the diamonds and rubies?"

"Ah, you have exquisite taste, Lord Vael." The goldsmith displayed the piece for Titus's perusal. "The rubies will compliment Lady Vael's brown eyes and hair."

"I will take it." Titus gathered the jewels.

After settling his account with Hammett, Titus secured the items, gained his saddle, and steered for Tharnham and his woman.

Gazing at the clouds, he plotted the delicious occupation of his tempting young bride's sumptuous territory and veered onto the verge. As he rounded a curve, six hooded riders ambushed him.

"Behold, the De Wolfe dog." One raider drew a sword. "It is time to avenge Lord Vael and Petroc Burville."

"Then you should have brought more men, as this is hardly a fair fight." In an instant, Titus unsheathed his Damascus blades, slid from his stallion, and slapped the beast's flank. Surrounded, he spread his legs and bent his knees to center himself, more amused than concerned. "Who wants to be first?"

"I will meet your challenge." A gadling charged,

and Titus merely sidestepped the unfortunate and clumsy fool. "Hold still, De Wolfe."

"You will have to do better, if you intend to best me." Titus shifted, hunkered, and evaded two attackers, whose voices he recognized as belonging to the elder sons of his miners. "No warning? Whither is the sport in that, good sirrahs?"

"You mock us, De Wolfe." Another spat. "You come to our lands, you take our women, and you steal our heritage. For that, you must die."

"Permit me to correct you," he said, as he confronted three assailants. "Your people waged war against His Majesty, and they lost the battle. As the victor, the King awarded me a single woman, an estate with large debts, and six great abysses of unknowing. Now, as I am anxious to return to my bride, I shall deal with you, but I will not kill you."

Moving swift and sure, he surrendered his weapons, punched a vagabond in the face, knocked two heads together, kicked a fourth would-be assaulter in the arse, and swept the remaining duo from their feet. As the idiots moaned, in unison, a compliment of soldiers, bearing the Vael standard, arrived.

"Lord Vael, are you wounded?" A guard waved a

signal, and the soldiers took the unfortunate band of rebels into custody. "Unmask them."

"Careful, and do not hurt them, as they knew not what trouble they courted." As Titus glimpsed those who would have dispatched him to the hereafter, he discovered they were, indeed, sons of some of his miners. "Send for Credan, and release the prisoners to their sires, that they may be disciplined." As he bent to gather his swords, he asked, "What brings you this way?"

"Hither we ventured by Lady Vael's command." The guard rubbed the back of his neck. "Her ladyship was quite displeased, which she made known to the entire garrison, that we allowed your lordship to depart Tharnham, unattended."

"Oh, she was?" He chuckled, as he checked to ensure the jewels remained in his leather pouch. "Never fear, as I will make amends, on your behalf." Whistling, he summoned his destrier, leaped into the saddle, and set a course for home, with the compliment of guards in his wake.

To save time, he abandoned the roads in favor of the shorter route through the valleys. After cutting across the south moorlands, he spied the frieze-carved parapets of Tharnham, and his blood stirred. When he entered the main gates, he slowed to a canter, and he bit his tongue against a snort of mirth, as he spied Rosenwyn, standing in the bailey.

With arms folded in front of her, her foot tapped a steady rhythm, reminiscent of the pose his mother adopted when she was vexed with his father. Ah, his lady truly cared for him.

"Good morrow, sweetheart." Ravenous for her supple flesh, he jumped from the saddle, grabbed the leather pouch, and marched straight to Rosenwyn, to steal a kiss.

Instead, she slapped him.

"How dare you leave Tharnham, without a contingent of guards?" Then she shoved him, and he vowed he would make love to her until she screamed again. "You could have been hurt or—worse. And I woke, alone and cold, in our bed." It was then she spotted the attackers, and she shrieked. "What happened?"

"I had a minor misunderstanding on the way home, when six raiders attacked me." As he tried to divert her, she evaded him. "Rosenwyn, prithee, my dear, let us retire to the solar."

"I see you, Marrak. And you, too, Gwennel." She

shook a fist. "I know all of you, and I will speak with your mothers. What gives you the right to harm Lord Vael, the man whose life is dearer to me than my own? The knight I love?" That ensnared his full attention, and he moved into action. "I shall have recompense."

"Vennor, send word to Credan that I cannot meet, today." After the steward acknowledged the directive, Titus wound an arm about Rosenwyn's waist, hugged her to his chest, and carried her to the main residence, but he paused at the double doors and shouted over his shoulder. "Tell him I will see him on Wednesday."

"Titus, put me down." She squirmed, and he swatted her bottom, in play. "Whither are you taking me?"

"To bed." He shuffled her in his hold. "Whither I shall put all this fire and spirit to good use."

"But I thought you had something to discuss with Credan, regarding the estate." His bride pouted, and he nipped her nose. "Is it not a matter of importance?"

"Nay, love. *This* is important, and I intend to keep you locked in our chambers, until the morrow." He grinned. "Mayhap, a sennight."

"Wherefore?" With her tongue, she teased the crest of his ear. "I am going nowhere, and you hold my heart, wherever you journey."

"And that is cause for a celebration." He ascended the stairs, as the thrill of victory charged his loins. "Because I have long coveted your heart."

"I thought you coveted my—" Given her bashful demeanor, in regard to marital relations, it appeared she could not bring herself to speak the word aloud, so she whispered it to him.

"That, too."

⇶⤜⤛

ROLLING ONTO HER back, Rosenwyn caught her breath, after her husband exercised her thoroughly, as was his way, not that she complained, extended an arm, and peered at the gold bracelet, with the shimmering wolf's head pendant dangling from the exquisite chain.

"Aside from your declaration, this is the most precious gift you have ever given me, as it marks me as a De Wolfe, for all to see." Titus shifted on his side and cupped her breast, and she sighed. "I will never take it off, not even when I bathe, as your mother does the same."

"You know of the De Wolfe custom, in regard to our brides?" She knew much more than that, but she would not tell him. When she nodded, he arched a brow. "Who told you?"

"Your mother met with me, prior to our nuptials." She recalled the startling conversation, in detail, as it was most provoking in its mastery of all things De Wolfe related, but she would never admit everything. "It was quite fascinating."

"To what purpose?" He eased atop her, pressed his hips to hers, nudged apart her legs, and rested between her thighs, in his much-professed new favorite position, and who was she to deny him? "And what did she say?"

"It was most arresting, as I gather she wanted to assess my dedication to the sacrament, and I do not blame her." She trailed her tongue along his beauteous lips, which never failed to stimulate him. "Isobeau loves you, and I do not believe she would have allowed our marriage ceremony to take place, had I not satisfied her requirements. And I have it on good authority that Desiderata did the same with Senara."

"Ah, a De Wolfe warrior demands an equally spirited bride." If only to soften his pride, she mused, and she tittered, as he rubbed her nose with his. "And you meet that requirement, as well as a few others, which only our men can define, and to which our women remain blissfully ignorant, to my inexpressible gratitude."

"I would not be too certain about that." When he frowned, she laughed. "In fact, I would assert that De Wolfe brides are just as knowledgeable as their husbands." As he nuzzled her neck, she closed her eyes and savored his tender affection. "Perchance, more so."

"Oh?" In that moment, Titus flinched, and she came alert. "Prithee, what do you mean?"

"Did you know that the reason Atticus always requests an estampie is because that is the only dance he has mastered?" Then she whispered, "And because your mother's bosom bounces, as she makes the rotations, and it inspires him, but she is not supposed to notice that."

"Oh, no." In haste, he retreated, winced, and shook his head. "Nay, Rosenwyn. I do not wish to hear such things of my mother, as that is too much to bear."

"And she insists that, for all their bravery and bluster, De Wolfe men possess a softer side, which they reveal only to their wives, and in that I agree." Indeed, that gem of information posited a cherished truth, as in private Titus fulfilled Rosenwyn's every need, with gentleness of which she never would have thought him capable. "Did you know that Atticus sings to your mother?"

"What?" Titus blanched. "Nay, anything but that. Say it is not so."

"My poor knight, it is most undeniably so. Wherefore does that bother my warrior, when you have faced death countless times?" When Titus pressed a palm to his belly and groaned, she burst into unrestrained mirth. "According to Isobeau, your father is blessed with the voice of a nightingale."

"No more." Venting something akin to a wild beast, Titus shuddered and covered his ears. "Prithee, no more, as I may never be able to look my father in the eye, again."

"Are you so delicate?" Sitting on her ankles, in bed, she assumed a mock pout. "Because, as Isobeau rightly proclaims, only a knight of incomparable strength is confident enough to admit he is not infallible and is secure enough in his manhood to share his vulnerabilities with his wife." Then she inclined her head. "And whether or not you like it, you are no different, and I love you."

"Am I not?" Facing her, in all his naked and aroused glory, Titus squared his shoulders. "How so?"

"Alas, must I list everything you do for me, in the confines of this room?" She flicked her fingers, and he joined her. "I should limit the recitation to my favored treat, which is when you hold me in your lap and feed me, by your own hands."

"But that is not so difficult a task." He stretched beside her and pulled her into his arms. "I do that because I love you, too."

"And that declaration, freely bestowed, marks you as the bravest, of all." Without warning, he pushed her to her back and covered her, and she trailed a finger along the curve of his jaw. "I also adore how you bathe me. Did you ever notice that you hum when you wash my back?"

In an instant, Titus stiffened his spine. "Promise me you will never tell my parents that."

EPILOGUE

The Lair

July

The Year of Our Lord, 1498

THE SHRILL CRY of a babe pierced the quiet, and the gathering of De Wolfes sighed, in unison, as the son of Arsenius and Senara announced his hunger with an impressive wail. As Senara tended the child, surrounded by De Wolfe wives, comparing their symbolic wolf's head bracelets, Titus patted Arsenius on the back.

"He is beauteous, cousin." How Titus longed to have a child with Rosenwyn, but despite his best efforts, and he gave it his all, every morrow and eventide, the blessing eluded them. "I am happy for you and Senara."

"Gramercy." Arsenius wiped a stray tear. "I am a father. Can you believe it? I never imagined how it would feel, and I am most content, as it is an awe-filled responsibility."

"Rosenwyn and I are honored that you asked us to stand for little Talan, at his baptism, and I must express my appreciation for the fact that you chose a name other than Titus." He laughed, though he envied his cousin. "Would that I might follow your example."

"No luck?" When Titus indicated the negative, Arsenius furrowed his brow and whistled. "Commiserations. But, from what Senara tells me, we had an advance start on you and Rosenwyn, not that I make sport of the situation, as the wait almost killed me."

"You believe you tell me something I know not?" When he recalled the lonely eventides spent in the stable, as he pleasured himself, Titus snorted. "My hand may never be the same."

"But I wager the work is satisfactory, now." Arsenius grinned. "Ah, my Senara is an ingénue of incomparable spirit."

"Rivaled only by my Rosenwyn, I suspect." In that moment, his lady glanced at him, and familiar warmth filled his senses. "It is good to be married, is it not?"

"Better than I ever presumed." Arsenius came alert. "He said something. Did you hear him?"

"He cooed." Father chucked Arsenius on the chin,

and he rushed to his son. "He is too young to speak, and you should enjoy this time of peace, as once he begins talking, it is doubtful he will ever stop."

"Is that the way of it?" Titus moved to the windows overlooking the bailey. "Because you always encouraged me."

"I never said I was a smart man." Papa speared his fingers through Titus's hair. "Now, when am I to be a grandfather?"

"Well, not yet." Huffing a breath, Titus shuffled his feet, because no matter how old he grew, his father still had a way of making his son feel like a gadling. "But I assure you it is not for lack of trying, and it will happen, sooner than later, I hope."

"Will you stop taunting him, as we cannot predict such delicacies of life." Mama elbowed Papa in the ribs. "My son, ignore your father, as he forgets his manners. And you should return to your chamber, as Rosenwyn requires your presence."

"But she is right—" It was then he noted her absence, and he scanned the solar. "Is something wrong? Is she ill?"

"Nay." Mama patted his cheek. "But you should go to her."

Titus nodded once and exited the solar. The corridor to his accommodation cut a path through the gallery, and he dipped his chin in insouciant salute to De Wolfes, past and present. Continuing down the hall, he navigated the home in which he grew up and reflected on all that had changed, since the boy became a man. Indeed, he was a different person, and he had Rosenwyn to thank for that. At the door to his room, the same one in which he spent his tender years, he paused to knock. Instead, he shoved open the panel.

"Hello." At the corner of the footboard, Rosenwyn loomed.

"Sweetheart." After securing the latch, he walked straight into her outstretched arms. "Are you unwell, my dear? Shall I summon the physic?"

"Nay." As she hugged him about the waist, she perched on her toes and bestowed upon him a tempting kiss. "I just wanted to—"

A chorus of cheers echoed through the castle, and Titus peered over his shoulder. "What is that?"

"I believe your mother shared my secret." His wife giggled. "I suspected she would not be able to contain herself, but that is understandable, given the importance."

"Rosenwyn, I am confused." When she trailed her tongue along the curve of his jaw, he groaned. "And now I am aroused."

"Then what say we celebrate the joyous occasion?" She gave him her back, and he loosened her laces. "After all, we will have little time to ourselves, once our new addition arrives."

"What are you talking about?" Then he surmised the motive behind her seduction. "My dear, is this about Petroc?" Titus rested fists on hips. "I told you, he performs an adequate service for Arsenius and Senara, and my cousin arranges a marriage, with a young woman from a good family. There is no reason to interfere in his life, as I am assured he is happy. Can you not fathom wherefore he does not wish to reside at Tharnham, when it was once his to inherit?"

"My foolish love." She dropped her gown and faced him. "This has naught to do with my brother, and I am happy for him, as he is content in his current station, and that is all I ever wanted. But you really do not know, do you? And your mother guessed ere we dined, last eventide."

"Guessed—what?" Another clamor interrupted his thought. "What do they herald?"

"The announcement of the next De Wolfe." Rosenwyn smiled. "Is it not wonderful?"

"You mean Arsenius and Senara expect another babe, already?" When his bride burst into laughter, Titus scratched his head. And then it hit him. "You mean, us?"

She simply nodded.

"Oh, my sweet girl." Dropping to his knees, Titus bowed his head and wept. "It is the answer to my prayers, but I am left to consider whether or not I am sufficient to the task, as it is an extraordinary responsibility to sire a child."

"My love, prithee, do not cry, as this is glorious news, and I would mark the event, with you." Rosenwyn tipped his chin and kissed away his tears, and he wrapped his arms about her hips. "And you will teach our son to hunt, to manage the estate, to respect women, and to honor the De Wolfe legacy."

"In that I will not fail." Standing, he lifted her in his embrace.

"Of course, not." She pressed her lips to his, as he carried her to bed. "But most important of all, you will teach him to be a great man, just like his father."

A NOTE FROM BARBARA DEVLIN

Dear Reader,

This book is a companion to the previous installment in the Heirs of Titus De Wolfe series. Tall, Dark & De Wolfe is told in the same timeline as The Big Bad De Wolfe (BBD). I never planned to tell the younger Titus's story, but so many of you contacted me after I published BBD that Kat told me I had to write the book. You may notice some overlapping dialogue in the first two scenes, which are rewritten from Titus's POV, because portions of those scenes occurred in BBD, so they had to match in this story. As for the length, I often receive complaints that my Kindle World titles are too short. You may not realize it, but Amazon contracts the Kindle World titles written for specific launches. Amazon determines the length and date of the release and then pays upfront money. While I would love to write longer De Wolfe tales, I am bound by the terms of the contract I sign with Amazon. In any case, I hope you enjoy my latest book, involving those loveable warrior knights, the De Wolfes.

Enjoy,
~Barb

ABOUT BARBARA DEVLIN

USA Today Bestselling, Amazon All-Star author Barbara Devlin was born a storyteller, but it was a weeklong vacation to Bethany Beach, DE that forever changed her life. The little house her parents rented had a collection of books by Kathleen Woodiwiss, which exposed Barbara to the world of romance, and Shanna remains a personal favorite. Barbara writes heartfelt historical romances that feature flawed heroes who may know how to seduce a woman but know nothing of marriage. And she prefers feisty but smart heroines who sometimes save the hero, before they find their happily ever after. Barbara earned an MA in English and continued a course of study for a Doctorate in Literature and Rhetoric. She happily considered herself an exceedingly eccentric English professor, until success in Indie publishing lured her into writing, full-time, featuring her fictional knighthood, the Brethren of the Coast.

Connect with Barbara Devlin at BarbaraDevlin.com, where you can sign up for her newsletter, The Knightly

News. And you can find a complete list of books on Barbara's Amazon Author Page.

Facebook: facebook.com/BarbaraDevlinAuthor

Twitter: @barbara_devlin